HIDDEN IN THE PRISM

BY
PATRICIA ANN KIRBY

PublishAmerica
Baltimore

© 2008 by Patricia Ann Kirby.
All rights reserved. No part of this book may be reproduced, stored in a retrieval system or transmitted in any form or by any means without the prior written permission of the publishers, except by a reviewer who may quote brief passages in a review to be printed in a newspaper, magazine or journal.

First printing

All characters in this book are fictitious, and any resemblance to real persons, living or dead, is coincidental.

PublishAmerica has allowed this work to remain exactly as the author intended, verbatim, without editorial input.

ISBN: 1-4241-8211-5 (softcover)
ISBN: 978-1-4489-7184-8 (hardcover)
PUBLISHED BY PUBLISHAMERICA, LLLP
www.publishamerica.com
Baltimore

Printed in the United States of America

To Marguerite, love, Patti

**Dedicated to my Godparents,
Aunt Lucille and Uncle Willard Kuchar**

Patricia A Kirby

Acknowledgments

I would like to thank my mom for everything she's done. Also, thanks to my family for being there for me. To my son, Paul Oliver, thank you for helping with my computer requirements. To Melinda, Paul's wife, thanks for helping edit this story in spite of your busy schedule, having three young children to care for during this time. Thanks to my daughter, Michelle Landvik, for her guidance. I could not have done this without their help.

Thank you to Vincent Kirby for his legal advice and to Frank Ritter for his publishing expertise during the contract stages of this project.

To my friends in this community, for their encouragement and support. I truly thank you all.

I also would like to thank PublishAmerica. During the editing process, a long illness and then a death in my family held up the timely process of completing this manuscript. Thank you to the publisher, for all of your patience and understanding.

Regards,
Patricia Ann Kirby

Wednesday, 12:45 p.m.

Annie was twelve years old, soon to be thirteen. With summer waning, she was getting tired of the days dragging in time. She decided it would be good for school to start again. The monotony of life in the small town of Battle Fork meant she and her friends had already spent many idle hours reading or using the computer at the library. She planned to go there again today, but on this particular day her trip to the library would change her life forever.

The day began like any other. She got up at about 9 a.m., took a shower, and ate breakfast. She helped her little sister Hannah wash and put away the dishes. Annie vacuumed, and then swept the floor in her home's entryway. Annie's last chore for the morning was to wash one window (it was window washing week) and today she cleaned the window of the upstairs' bathroom. Once her chores were finally finished, Annie ate an egg salad sandwich for lunch with her mom and Hannah. Her brother Jonah had yet to return from camping with a friend and his family. With her sister responsible for cleaning up after lunch, Annie finally had her free time. Impatient to have some fun, Annie walked to the garage to get her bike, only to find the back tire completely flat. Instead of looking for the air pump or walking her bike to the gas station to get it fixed, she decided to take her brother's bike to the library.

Annie rode down the driveway and turned south towards the library. Wanting to get more mileage from her minutes, she stood up on the pedals, using her full weight to move the clunky boy's bike as fast as possible. She sped along the quiet street, happy to be alive this fine day, her hair blowing in the wind, when suddenly the pedals spun out from under her feet and her pelvic bone slammed into the bar of her brother's bike. "Ouch!" Annie yelped, her pain excruciating. She held on to the handlebars and narrowly avoided a collision course with the hot July pavement. Annie was miserable and embarrassed. She painfully coasted the bike to a stop and got off, blinking back tears, trying to look inconspicuous. She didn't want people to see her crying like a baby. Trying to act as though nothing had happened, she bent down to re-attach the chain. Her fingers fumbled with the gears and the chain. She glanced up at the plate glass window near where she knelt, to scan the reflection in Bud's Hardware store window. She wanted to make sure no one witnessed her embarrassing accident. Just as she was about to return her attention to the bike chain, she noticed movement in the glass's reflection.

Just as she was about to return her attention to the bike chain, she noticed movement in the glass's reflection.

She blinked again, the tears still in her eyes. Yikes! An animal or something was reflected in the glass. It traveled along the curb of the street near her. Mesmerized, she stared at the creature's outline. She'd never seen such a strange thing! Annie wasn't sure what it was, but whatever it was, it looked hideous. The body resembled a rat, but its size was closer to a badger. Its ears, nose, front paws, and part of the cheeks were hairless. It had a long thin nose, pointed at the end, like a mosquito stinger, with a few hairs growing on it. Under its chin was something like a scraggly beard. Its mouth curled into a sneering scowl. The creature walked upright, traveling nearby Annie, unaware of her stares.

"Eww! What a gross-looking rat!" Annie thought, but soon realized it only looked similar. As the creature came closer, Annie recoiled. A horrible stench filled the air, like rotting meat and sweat. It smelled even worse than the squirrel that got stuck and died in the vent on her family's roof a couple of years back. It was awful! She gagged, gulped air, and gasped. Fear suddenly hit Annie. Would this ugly rat creature hurt her? Her gasp drew the creature's attention. He turned his head towards her in the glass reflection. He stiffened when he saw her looking back at him. The creature dropped to all four paws and scampered under a parked car, his head turning to keep Annie in his sights. His eyes betrayed contempt for the wiry blond. Annie whipped her head around to stare directly at the spot where she'd seen the thing reflected in the glass. The creature wasn't there!

Puzzled, Annie turned back to the windowpane. She still could see the creature making its way along the road further down. It rounded the corner and ran down the side street and out of view. As quickly as she was able, Annie put the chain back on the gear, hopped on the bike and headed the same direction as the creature. Curiosity consumed her. She rode down a residential street, looking down each driveway and scanning the bushes in the yards as she passed. Soon the street ended in a dead end. Beyond the tree-lined street Annie noticed a small creek that wound through dense trees and brush towards the edge of town. Annie circled around, eying the yards, hoping to get another look at the little beast and then headed back in the direction she had come.

By this time Annie forgot about hurting herself on her brother's bike. She was intent on spotting the creature. She spent another fifteen minutes riding around the area, scanning every alley and storm drain. Annie stopped in front of Bud's Hardware, not only hot and tired, but also disappointed. "It was no use," she thought. Whatever she saw was gone.

Even though she had no luck spotting the creature, Annie's newly kindled desire for adventure brought a smile to her face. Questions started pumping through her head, "What kind of creature was that and why could I only see the animal when I looked into the glass's reflection?" Hopefully, the library could provide her with some much needed information.

Annie parked her brother's bike at the library's bike rack, ran up the steps and pushed open the front door. There was a hush as she entered the library. Annie walked over to the water fountain, just inside the entrance near the bathrooms, and took a long cold drink of water. The first thing she wanted to do was call her friend Maggie.

"I wish I had a cell phone right now! Half of the kids in my class have their own, but not me," Annie silently whined. "Oh well." She took a coin from her pocket and dropped it into the telephone in the library foyer.

"Hello?"

"Maggie! It's me, Annie. You've got to come over here to the library right away! You'll never believe what I just saw! It was the ugliest thing I've ever seen in my life!" Satisfied that Maggie's curiosity would get the best of her, Annie hung up and waited impatiently for Maggie to arrive.

All of the computers were busy. Annie looked at the sign-up sheet and wrote her name next to the first open space at 2:30.

Realizing that just waiting would be of no help in reaching her goal, Annie began scanning the bookshelves, looking for a section that might have a book about weird animals. Annie found herself in the very back corner of the library. When she backed up a little to read the titles of the books higher up on a shelf, Annie's eyes focused on a volume that looked promising. Using a chair, she climbed up and took a closer look. The book was titled, Ancient Legends, Strange Wives Tales, and Stories from Our Fathers. It was so old its pages were yellowed and crisp. When she lifted open the leather cover, the book smelled like moth balls and mildew. "Ugh!" she gasped. The book's smell put her off, but the title intrigued her. "Where else could I look to research that thing I've just seen?" she thought, "It was too weird, especially since I couldn't see the creature with my naked eye." Annie carried the massive book to a nearby table. She sat down in the back corner at the old table and carefully opened the thick cover. She began to page through the big volume.

The book was hand printed and illustrated. Annie carefully turned the pages, feeling as though she'd discovered a special treasure. She turned randomly to a page and found a watercolor illustration of the earth surrounded by ice in the atmosphere, like a shield, around the whole planet. On the earth below, she could make out animals of all kinds were entering an ark. "Noah's ark," Annie thought.

The earth was enveloped by a thick layer of ice
in the very beginning, like a greenhouse.

The caption on the illustration read: *"The earth was enveloped by a thick layer of ice in the very beginning, like a greenhouse." Giants lived on the earth at that time.* Mankind also populated the warm, misty lands and built large cities, but evil abounded.

"God saw how evil the people were. The first sin in the Garden of Eden had contaminated the population, and the earth had become an abominable wasteland of violence, corruption, and wickedness. God was sad. Out of all of the humans on the whole planet, only one walked with God. God found favor with Noah. He told Noah to build a big ark out of gopher wood. God provided the knowledge and supplies for making the ark, and told Noah and his family to gather up pairs of birds and animals from the earth."

Annie was fascinated! She had read the story in Bible School, but in this book, there was an illustration of a comet or meteor flying through the heavens above, ready to break the shield that surrounded the earth. She studied the drawing. Pairs of giraffes, rats, snakes, a ram, and sheep were in line to enter the ship. If one looked closely, three men could be seen on the ship. "They must be part of Noah's family," Annie thought. The artist had identified Noah showing his name on a nearby mailbox.

"After Noah, his family, and all the animals were inside the ark, God shut the door. And then it began to rain. The comet collided with the thick layer of ice in the atmosphere. The falling shards of ice melted and it rained for 40 days and nights, flooding the earth. Noah and his family would remain in the ark for several months, waiting for the floodwaters to recede. The covering which had prevented a rainbow from being visible on the earth had now been eliminated. Direct sunlight could now pass through drops of rain, creating a rainbow. God made a promise with Noah and his descendants to never destroy humankind with a flood again. The rainbow represented God's promise.

"The earth now rotated in the heavens with full exposure to the elements. Cold and hot weather patterns became part of life on the planet-from ice and snow-covered mountain caps to heat scorched desert floors."

Annie was enthralled by the story. Turning away from the book for a moment, she noticed a sign that she hadn't seen before. On it Annie read these words:

THIS SECTION OF THE LIBRARY IS RESTRICTED. NO VOLUMES ARE TO BE TAKEN OUT ON LOAN. DO NOT USE THESE BOOKS WITHOUT AUTHORIZATION.

Annie wished she hadn't seen the notice. Now she felt guilty looking at this book. She didn't put the book back though, but instead carefully turned the page. On the left hand side was an engraving of a dragon with fire coming from his nostrils as he attacked a crusader valiantly fending him off. A castle loomed in the distance on a hill. There was a long narrow road and a drawbridge leading to the castle behind the pair in battle. She loved the artwork, and was studying the drawing when she heard someone coming. She looked up to see who it was, hoping her guilty feelings would not be easily recognizable on her face. Luckily, it was Maggie.

Maggie pulled up a chair next to her and asked eagerly, "What's up?" Annie gestured for her to be as quiet as possible. She pointed at the notice and then back at the book before her. She whispered to Maggie the story about her brother's slipped bike chain and the ugly creature that was invisible when she tried to look directly at it. She explained how she could see its reflection when she looked at it in the window pane. With the sign in the back of their minds, the girls' whispered back and forth over the day's events.

Eventually, they quieted down and being very quiet, paged through the book. Carefully scanning the parchment pages, they looked for clues. The sound of someone's approach caught Annie's attention. An old woman with a scowl on her face walked up to their table.

"What are you doing here?" she asked as she pointed at the sign. She waited for a response. When none was given she began to speak, "What on earth are you looking for? This area is restricted! You shouldn't be back here, girls." The old woman's scolding tone was frightening. "The book you have is very delicate, as are all of the volumes in this section. We plan to set up a special room for these rare and valuable books, but as of now, we have only this sign and the remoteness of the area to keep the general public from using these titles."

An old woman with a scowl on her face walked up to their table.

Annie stammered. "I'm sorry. I was trying to find some information about a creature I saw today. I hoped there would be something about it in this old book."

"What are you talking about, young lady?" asked the librarian. A look of surprise was quickly replaced by an impatient glower that emphasized her already wrinkly face. It was evident through her expression she had a dislike for Annie.

"Have you ever heard of an animal that looks like a rat, except it has skin on its face and paws, a scraggly beard and a long stinger-shaped nose, like a mosquito? It was over a foot tall. It could stand up on its back legs, or run on all fours. It had three barbs on its tail, like a little pitchfork. I saw one today. I looked in the window and I could see it scampering along the curb."

The woman just stared at Annie for a long moment then she walked over to the table and removed the book. The tall woman reached up and pushed the volume back into its place. She looked at Annie and said, "You have an active imagination, miss. There are no such things as invisible animals. I have never heard of such a silly notion, and I believe that the summer has left you with far too much time to dream up stories in your mind. Now, both of you go over to the adventure section and try reading a Nancy Drew book or one of the other stories in that area. The items in this section are for special use only."

The girls stood, turned, and headed for the door. Annie no longer felt like reading. When they got outside, Annie was upset. Maggie could read Annie's expression and tried to brighten her mood by exclaiming, "I got my allowance today. Do you want to get a pop? Let's go to the Snack Shop. We can talk about this and get rid of the rotten feeling the librarian gave us. I bet she wouldn't have talked like that to my mom or dad."

Annie checked the chain on the bike before they rode to the burger shop. Maggie ordered two drinks and an order of fries for them to share. After the order came up, Maggie paid for it and brought the food over to the outdoor table under a shade tree. Annie got ketchup and a couple of straws and napkins. They relished the hot French fries and sipped on their drinks.

"Today hasn't gone very well but this really hits the spot!" said Annie. She smiled at Maggie, but remembering her recent unpleasant ordeal spouted, "That library lady wouldn't even listen to me. And she was so mean!"

Maggie nodded empathetically and then her face brightened. "Oh, I almost forgot! I was going to tell you something today anyway! Yesterday, I was at my Cousin Michelle's house and we were in the yard picking those dinky little flowers that have the tiny little butterflies and bees flying around them. All of a sudden I noticed my watch was missing! I knew I had it on when I got there! Michelle tried to help me find it. We looked and looked. I was getting worried because Michelle and I got matching watches last Christmas from our grandmother so I didn't want to lose it. We wandered around the front and back yard looking for it.

"Suddenly, I heard someone call out to me from the neighbor's house. On the porch I saw a lady about my mom's age. She was sitting in a rocking chair, reading a book. She smiled at me and said, 'The watch you are looking for, Maggie, is beside the front steps on the left side, hanging on a branch near the ground.' I asked her how she knew my name and the lady gestured at me to look for it, then added, 'Get the watch, then come back over.'

"I went to the front yard and looked where she said the watch would be, and it was there! I asked my cousin about the woman and she told me Ms. Nichols has lived next door to her all of her life. Michelle said that the woman used to babysit her when she was younger, but some of the neighbors thought her odd. She told me she thinks Ms. Nichols is nice, and doesn't care what the neighbors think. So Michelle and I went back to the woman. I asked Ms.

Nichols, 'How did you know my name and where I could find my missing watch? In fact, how did you know my watch was missing?' Ms. Nichols answered, 'It's something that has happened since my childhood. Sometimes things just pop into my head. I don't control when it happens. I saw you looking for something in the yard and knew what you wanted.'"

Maggie finished her summary. "At the library a little while ago, I was thinking that she was the exact opposite of the librarian. We should talk to her about the thing you saw."

Annie smiled. "I would be happy to find anyone who could help me figure out what I saw and smelled! I know I didn't dream it up." Annie smiled at her friend and realized how tired she was from the events of the day.

It was time to go home. The girls rode together. Annie said goodbye to Maggie at the end of the street, and pulled into her driveway just as her dad arrived. She put the bike in the garage. He greeted her. "One of the men in the office said he saw you fixing your bike chain today."

"I wanted to go to the library, but my bike tire was flat so I used Jonah's bike. The chain came off next to the hardware store. I hurt myself but I'm OK. While I was fixing the chain, I saw a rat or something in the reflection of the store window. I tried to look right at it but I couldn't see it. When I looked in the reflection in the window again I could see it! What could it have been?" Father and daughter both headed into the house together.

"Honey, I don't know what you saw, but if you are like most girls, you wouldn't want to see a rat!" He playfully messed up her hair and turned to go into the living room to watch the evening news. That night the family sat around the dinner table when Annie's dad asked, "Did anybody else see an ugly creature today? Annie came across a monster rat when she was riding Jonah's bike." Annie's brother and sister both shook their heads, wide eyed at their dad's remark.

Annie felt sure her dad was making a joke about what she had confided to him. She told her brother Jonah about using his bike and the incident that followed. He laughed and gave his dad a grin. Hannah didn't laugh. She made a gesture with her nose in response to the stench that followed in the rat thing's wake. She said she was glad she didn't see it. Hannah was two years younger than Annie and didn't have an adventurous side. She was more into nail polish and Barbie Dolls.

Annie's mom gave her husband a look that said not to tease Annie. As a mother she knew that Annie was sensitive to jokes with her in it and hated it. As usual, Annie felt misunderstood. She was anxious for tomorrow to come so she could see Maggie's cousin's neighbor. After being scowled at by the librarian and kidded by her family, Annie hoped Ms. Nichols would be of help.

Annie and her sister did the dishes. They went to the living room and Annie tried to watch television for awhile, but she was too preoccupied. She was also achy from her injury on the bike. She asked her mom for a couple of aspirin, brushed her teeth and went to bed.

As Annie stretched out, she stared at the ceiling and wondered what the heck she'd seen that afternoon. She decided to try to draw a picture of it. She sat at the desk in her bedroom and wrote down everything she remembered about the event. She drew how the thing looked when it was standing and what it looked like when it ran on all fours. She made a little map of where it was when she spotted it. Exhausting her memory of each and every detail of the encounter, Annie clicked off the light and, after tossing and turning for awhile, fell asleep.

Thursday, 7:49 a.m.

The light streamed through the window. Annie opened her eyes, but it took a minute to remember the big plan she made with Maggie. The night before, she asked her mom and dad if she could go to Maggie's cousin's house. "It wasn't that far, especially on bikes," She thought. Annie planned to walk her bike first to the service station to get it fixed, especially after what had happened on Jonah's bike. Until now, the summer had been dragging along, but now time felt different. Annie wanted to explore the event of yesterday as quickly as possible. She washed the breakfast dishes and finished her other chores before she dug out a thin backpack and slipped her journal into it. She then called Maggie.

Soon, they were walking their bikes to the service station. They bought a pop and drank it while Jake, the service station attendant, patched Annie's bike tire. After the tire was fixed they rode their bikes to Michelle's house.

When Annie and Maggie got there, they told Michelle what had happened to Annie the previous day. "I told Annie about your neighbor," Maggie said. "I think Annie should ask Ms. Nichols about it. If anyone could tell her something, your neighbor probably could!" Michelle called her neighbor to see if they could come over for a visit. The girls walked across the yard to the steps of the neighbor's screened porch. Annie saw a telescope, some petrified rocks and a big shard of crystal near an old rocking chair. There was a reading table with books and a magnifying glass lying on top of the pile. The tinkle of wind chimes made a magical sound as it swung gently in the breeze. Michelle rang the doorbell.

A woman Annie suspected to be in her early forties opened the door and greeted the three. Michelle introduced the woman to Annie as Ms. Nichols and then explained that Annie wanted to talk to her about the strange thing she saw yesterday. Ms. Nichols invited them in. She led them to the den where they took seats around a big old table. A strong-looking, tiger-striped cat wandered into the den, flicking his tail as he studied the newcomers. Ms. Nichols picked him up and said, "This is Tiggy, or Tiggs, as I sometimes call him. He is such good company!" She smiled at the visitors and said, "Hang on-I'll get us all something to drink." She left the room.

The girls looked around the cozy den. It was filled with bookshelves. There was an early model radio and record player enclosed in a tall standing cabinet. Ms. Nichols returned within a few minutes with a tray of glasses filled with ice cold lemonade. She passed the drinks around and settled into her chair. "Tell me, Annie, what brings you here today?"

Annie began by telling Ms. Nichols about the bike accident. Everyone was very attentive as she carefully detailed the events of the previous day. Annie had brought along her journal and showed Ms. Nichols the drawings she had made the previous night. Ms. Nichols asked Annie, "Did you say you had tears in your eyes when you saw the creature?"

"It hurt so bad I couldn't help it!" Annie answered.

Ms. Nichols replied, "I believe what happened is that you saw into a dimension usually invisible to humans, but visible to you because of the circumstances of your accident. Ironically, if you would have asked me about this creature two days ago, I would have nothing to offer you other than a vague recollection of my dad talking about them. However, just the other day I brought several boxes of books given to me by my father from our family farm to my house here in town. I was paging through one of the books just yesterday that had to do with this subject. Hold on-I'll go get it!"

Ms. Nichols left the room for a few minutes and returned with an old book and several prisms. Placing the prisms on the table, she opened the book to a page she had marked. On the left hand page was an illustration of the animal Annie had seen. It had a rat-like head, with longer ears and an extremely long stinger-shaped nose. It had wisps of whiskers around its jaw and under the nose. Scraggy hairs grew randomly about the face. At the top of the head was a crop of hair that grew like a tuft grass from a peak. The rest of the body was covered with fur, except for the pot-belly and parts of the gnarled hands and feet. The creature had a strange rat tail with three prongs at the end, each capped with an arrow tip, like a little pitchfork. The caption at the bottom of the illustration read: *"The Zorg. This creature has co-existed with mankind since time began. It is invisible to the human eye. It is considered a minion of the Devil."* The illustration showed an elf accompanied by a cat, chasing the zorg. The illustration appeared to depict the middle ages, as the city had cobblestone streets. The girls studied the illustration. The idea that these things might exist sent a chill through Annie.

Ms. Nichols read the opposite page. *"Zorgs are once again growing in numbers, giving the elves more evil than they can alone contain. The elves are employing cats and other animals of the earth in their efforts to control the zorg population. Being invisible to the human eye, zorgs have few natural enemies in the earthly realm. Their numbers increase at various times throughout history, especially during crises.*

"The zorgs' primary mission is to harvest as many souls as possible. They desire the ruination of humanity. Zorgs create confusion and chaos and have been rightfully accused of acts of arson, malaria epidemics, running off livestock, food poisoning, and other terrible crimes. They welcome natural

disasters. They strive to anguish the human soul in hopes that the human soul rejects God's comfort.

"Zorgs offer these souls-in-ruin the opportunity to actively participate in the evil deeds of the zorg network, initially through prompting thoughts of despair and revenge. The zorgs then hook these humans into their service to inflict physical and emotional suffering amongst their peers, with the ultimate goal of increasing the zorg following.

"Cats can vaguely make out a zorg's shape if the light is right, although it is purported that a zorg's awful smell strongly pervades both dimensions, especially for a cat's fine sense of smell. It is believed that placing a prism on the collar of a cat gives the cat the ability to see a zorg clearly. The human eye can detect the presence of a zorg when using a prism to view the surroundings. .

"One of the greatest men of the scientific community, Galileo, discovered the creatures long ago. He was working on a new telescope when he fell into a deep sleep, exhausted from his tedious efforts. While he slept, a zorg crept through the window on a mission to destroy Galileo's work. Zorgs dread and try to thwart intellectual advancement. They prefer humanity to remain in bondage to fear and ignorance, rather than acquiring the knowledge that brings Truth into the light."

While he slept, a zorg crept through the window on a mission to destroy Galileo's work.

HIDDEN IN THE PRISM

Ms. Nichols continued reading. *"As the zorg tiptoed across the table where Galileo slept, it bumped a telescope lens that was lying against a book. The lens clattered onto the table, waking Galileo. With one swift motion, Galileo grabbed the lens before it fell to the floor, to keep it from breaking. As he lifted the circular lens to see if there had been any damage to the thick glass along the edge, he could see movement in the lens. He turned to look about him, but could not see anything in the room moving. Looking closely again, he spotted a rat-type creature reflected in the cut edge. He picked up his prism, resting nearby, and looked through it to see if it reflected the image. He saw a creature so ugly and evil, Galileo froze with fear. The zorg looked straight at the man holding the prism, and then turned and scampered into a dark corner of the laboratory where he stood watching the man follow his movements. Galileo, a religious man, developed the habit of saying the Lord's Prayer throughout his life. It kept him grounded and gave him a sense of relief during the chaotic times. At this moment the words of this prayer sprang to his lips. 'Our Father, who art in heaven...' A transformation of the creature astonished Galileo as he looked on. The creature suddenly weakened. It was visibly tormented by the sound of the powerful prayer that was given to mankind by Jesus Christ. The zorg stumbled, knees weak. He glared at Galileo, gave out a hiss, and turned to the window, the pitchfork-shaped tip of the tail outlined by the candle light, as the creature disappeared from sight. Galileo saw it all, upside-down in the glass of the prism.*

"He named the slithering rat thing after a man named Zorg. Mr. Zorg had lost the girl of his dreams to Galileo. This maiden, Marina Gamba, later became Galileo's lover and the mother of his three children. Mr. Zorg detested Galileo and took great pleasure attempting to cause Galileo's demise, with unseen

deeds, lies and back-stabbing, taking every opportunity to sabotage Galileo and his work. Naming the newly discovered creatures after Mr. Zorg was the only vengeance that Galileo ever took against the man that haunted his existence."

"Galileo's conscience clearly directed him to tell others of this threat. However, he was advised by a network of his true friends to lay low with this knowledge. They could not guarantee that this was not just another late night hallucination after spending many hours alone in his study, and others in the scientific community would seize this opportunity to discredit any of Galileo's work. Disappointed but undaunted, Galileo pursued his study of zorgs alone. Perhaps his greatest discovery was the direct link between increased zorg activity and times of great sickness or political unrest."

Ms. Nichols continued. "Later in life, Galileo again tried to warn the world about zorgs. He distributed a paper entitled, Zorgs: A Threat to Humanity, and prisms to anyone who would take them in the scientific and church communities. A few of these intellectuals, after reading this report, were astonished at Galileo's hypothesis that such dark creatures really exist. In order to keep people from panicking, the 'powers that be' denied any knowledge or existence of zorgs, allowing the information to fade into oblivion. Only a few references to the zorgs remain."

Spellbound, Annie looked back at the drawing on the left page of the old book. Her eyes soaked in every detail. Maggie said, "What a neat book you got from your dad! It is a little scary, though. Annie and I tried to find something about this subject at the library yesterday, but the librarian wouldn't let us look."

Ms. Nichols told the girls, "My dad was a history professor. Early in his life he traveled, studying at many universities around the world. He spoke at different colleges and universities about early civilizations, and I went with him when I wasn't in school. He studied the most interesting things, collecting books, maps and unusual things from all over the world."

Ms. Nichols turned the page and continued. "Most people would never believe this stuff is actually a part of history. The institutions with this knowledge preferred to keep it to themselves. The institutions believed that only they were qualified to understand and disseminate knowledge. They held the reins. People were taught to read and accept only the books which had been 'approved.' Without all the truth, humans make decisions based on partial truths or ignorance. In this manner they could harness the fear, darkness, and ignorance of people to manipulate events to their own advantage.

"During the Renaissance," Ms. Nichols continued, "when the arts and sciences flourished, the public became more independent-thinking. The big institutions felt some of their control slipping away as education became more accessible to the working class. The elitists reacted by scoffing at their very own who spent any time teaching 'common folk.' Such discrimination prevented an even more widespread education of the masses. The dumb masses!" Ms. Nichols joked, grinning. She kept reading.

"The institutions were unable to disguise the truth altogether. They tried to hide it but it was like trying to take pepper out of a potato salad. Those who think clearly can use their reason and intellect to find the truth before their very eyes."

Ms. Nichols explained. "For example, we have known for centuries now that our earth is spherical, not flat. Aristotle noted that during a partial eclipse, the earth always cast a curved shadow on the moon, no matter one's location. However, most believed the world was flat because they'd always heard that it was, or never thought about it at all instead of thinking there is always something new to discover. Electricity was here on earth from the very beginning, although no one could see it unless they saw lightning. The cavemen didn't know that the power of electricity was there to harness. There are surely other wonders here on earth, right under our noses that exist as invisibly as electricity, only we have yet to discover them. People hate to change the way they think, and it takes a whole generation to pass, in most cases, before a new idea or thought is embraced by mankind." Annie, Maggie, and Michelle stood by the open book and looked at the illustration before Ms. Nichols closed the book.

It only makes sense to us now that the world is round, because all of the planets and the moon and sun are round, so who could picture the world as flat surrounded by round orbs in the heavens?

Ms. Nichols stood up to stretch for a minute. She smiled at Annie and the other girls. "Girls, it is funny how over the years I have collected prisms at sales and auctions. I think in light of recent events, I can part with a couple so that you may have your own. You might find them as useful as Galileo did."

"Wow!" all three said at once. Ms. Nichols walked over to the prisms she had brought into the room earlier. She handed one to each girl. Happily the girls accepted. They held their prisms up to their eyes. It was hard to hold the glass to see right-side up, but they learned to tilt the prism. "I am so glad to have met you," said Annie. "The librarian made me feel bad, but meeting you makes up for it. Thank you for listening to my story and giving us the prisms. I can hardly wait to try mine out!"

When they got up to leave they promised Ms. Nichols they would let her know if they discovered anything new. "The adventurous spirit is contagious." Annie thought. Ms. Nichols gave them her phone number before they left.

Annie and Maggie said goodbye to Michelle at her back door, then rode home. They spoke little as they pedaled, lost in their own thoughts. Before long they were back in their own neighborhood. Annie pulled the bike into the garage. She slid the thin backpack holding her journal off her shoulder and tapped her pocket to be sure she still had her new prism. She walked into the kitchen just as her mom, brother, and sister were gathered for lunch.

"Annie! You're home!" her mom greeted her. Annie greeted everyone and went to the sink to wash her hands. Her mom poured her a glass of milk and fixed her an egg salad sandwich. Annie's appetite suddenly kicked in seeing the food. When Annie's mom was done they said grace and began to eat lunch. As they ate, Annie told them about her morning and about meeting Ms. Nichols. Interrupting Annie, Annie's mom suddenly remembered to tell Annie, "The library called for you. Someone found your library card. You are supposed to pick it up."

HIDDEN IN THE PRISM

Annie thought, it must have fallen from her pocket while she was reading that book with Maggie, or maybe when she got out the money to make the phone call. She would go back there with Maggie and Michelle and at the same time, using their new prisms, they could all look for the zorg. Annie pulled her prism from her pocket and showed everyone the triangular bar of glass that Ms. Nichols had given her. Jonah reached over to touch it. "Cool!" he said to his sister after he looked through it, and then went back to eating his lunch. Hannah asked to look, too, and Annie held it out to her. Before long the sandwiches were gone and the dishes were cleared and washed. Annie's brother went out to mow, then to the pool at the park. Mom would drop off Hannah at the pool while running errands.

Annie called Maggie. "My mom said the library called here. I lost my library card and I'm supposed to pick it up. Want to go there with me to get it? Maybe you could ask Michelle to come, too. We can all try our prisms!" Maggie hung up and then called Michelle. About a half hour later she called back.

"Annie, I just got off the phone with Michelle. Her parents need to go out of town and Michelle asked if we could stay over with her from Friday afternoon until Sunday. Maybe we could wait until tomorrow morning to get your library card. We can check out our prisms then, too. Afterwards we can go to Michelle's. It'll be so fun! Do you think you can go? My mom already talked to my aunt and they came up with this plan together."

Annie replied, "I'll do my chores this afternoon and stick around home. Hopefully then my mom and dad will let me go. I'll have my mom talk to your mom."

Annie wanted to use her prism. She wanted to look for that creature with her friends tomorrow! In the mean time, she started to do every job she could see needed to be done. She started a load of laundry. She vacuumed the living room and dining room, then took the soft yellow cloth and dusted and polished all the furniture in the living room and dining room. When her mom returned from errands, the laundry was done, folded, put away, and the house gleamed and shined! Even her dad noticed the spotless house when he got home at dinnertime. That evening, not only did Annie get permission to spend the weekend at Michelle's after her mom spoke to Michelle's mom, but Annie's dad whipped out a ten dollar bill for her to spend! Annie was in heaven!

That night Annie told her dad about Ms. Nichols and showed him her prism. Annie was glad her dad hadn't brought up the bike incident, because she no longer needed to find someone to believe her story. Not many people would let her live it down if she told them about what she had learned this past couple of days.

Annie realized she was too excited to watch television. She went to her room. She pulled out a list she had made that afternoon after cleaning the house. She rummaged through her closet and dug out a gym bag and a sleeping bag. She re-rolled the sleeping bag into a neat, tidy bundle. She then unzipped the gym bag and pulled it open like jaws. She set items of clothes in piles on the bed, and one by one she stuffed everything into the bag. She stacked the sleeping bag and the gym bag in the corner.

Suddenly Annie remembered what she had wanted to do all afternoon. Annie grabbed her journal, secretly tucked away under her mattress, and recorded every detail about what Ms. Nichols said that she could remember. She spent some more time on her picture, and felt relief that the creature she saw the other day now had a name: Zorg. She could hardly wait for morning.

Friday, 8:11 a.m.

Annie woke to another nice day. She hopped out of bed in a big hurry. She was excited to try out her prism. She greeted her dad on his way out the door to work. He wished her a great time this weekend and said goodbye. Her mom insisted on making Annie toast and eggs before she left for the day. Before long Annie was walking towards Maggie's house. Maggie was waiting for her.

They headed down the sidewalk carrying their sleeping bags and overnight bags, one in each hand. They made their way to Michelle's house. Since they planned to look for the zorg with the prisms, they decided they should walk instead of bike when they would later pick up Annie's library card. Then they could search the area where Annie had seen the zorg.

Annie and Maggie dropped their gear on the porch near Michelle's back door and pushed the doorbell. Michelle led them in with their stuff and took Annie to meet her mom and dad. Her mom was busy preparing for their trip that afternoon, and was glad the girls had plans to go to the library so she could get her packing and other chores done unhampered by company.

The three girls were on their way to the library by ten that morning. Annie had always loved adventure, and this morning she felt full of excitement as they approached the spot where she had seen the zorg. It must have been a strange sight to see them walking down the sidewalk, each holding a prism to their eyes. So far the girls hadn't seen anything but the shimmer of rainbow surrounding every object.

"That creepy zorg must not be around today," Annie thought. Annie was disappointed. She very much wanted her friends to see the ugly creature.

Before long they were standing outside the old brick building of the library. No one had seen anything weird. It was getting warm as the girls walked up the steps and into the building. First they took turns at the ice cold water fountain, and then Annie walked to the front desk where a clerk sat at a computer terminal. Annie gave her name and asked for her library card. The clerk reached into a drawer and pulled out a card with a note clipped to it. She handed Annie her library card, and asked her to wait for a minute, if she wouldn't mind, until Mrs. Cain arrived. "Mrs. Cain wants to see you," the young clerk said.

The girls walked over to the nearest big table and sat down. Maggie asked Annie, "Who is Mrs. Cain?"

Annie shrugged her shoulders to answer, "No clue!" Annie was looking through the prism again, noticeably impatient. She wondered what Mrs. Cain wanted. They were wasting precious time on their first-ever zorg hunt.

The old librarian walked in. She walked to the counter with a paper bag and spoke to the clerk. She turned and looked towards the girls waiting at the table. Annie froze. "Not her!" Annie thought. Annie didn't want to talk to her. What did she want? Annie saw a chilly expression come over Mrs. Cain's face, but before the woman came towards the girls her expression became more like a forced smile. She looked down at Annie at the table, and said, "I was glad you left your card under the table where you were sitting the other day. I was tempted to call your parents and revoke your library privileges for not following the clear instructions to stay out of that part of the library. But don't think you are in the clear yet. The book you used has been damaged; there is a tear on the binding. And…" she paused and scanned Annie, "the book beside it was damaged, also. I hope you have the money to pay for the books to be repaired."

Once again Annie felt anger at this woman's manner and meanness. Annie hadn't touched any other books! Annie fumed, "Who did she think she was, anyway? Didn't the library belong to the public, and wasn't that woman paid by everyone's taxes? Well, our moms' and dads' taxes, at least? Besides, I knew we hadn't hurt the book we looked at. We were so careful!"

Annie refused to accept the accusation. "I don't know what you are talking about." She looked straight at Mrs. Cain and decided that she could be just as fierce in the face as that woman was, only maybe not as ugly. The stern woman's stare was chilling. Maggie and Michelle recoiled in their seats.

Annie leaned into her stare and spoke defiantly, "First of all, Mrs. Cain, I never saw the sign on the bookshelf when I began to look at that book. Secondly, I have spent a lot of hours at this library and I know how to turn the pages of books without doing damage. I know my friend and I didn't tear or hurt this book in any way. If those books are so important, maybe you should block off the area until you get them moved to a special room where people won't accidentally use them by mistake." The twelve-year-old tried to glare at her. "And for your information, we didn't touch any other books in that section."

Mrs. Cain turned her attention towards Maggie. "I know you girls tore that book, and you tore the other book in the same section. I spent time checking the other books, as well." Maggie was flustered by this accusation. Annie watched as Maggie squirmed and reddened in the face. Just then Annie's hand closed around the prism in her shorts' pocket. Reflexively, Annie held the prism to her eyes and looked at the woman before her. "How can I defend my friends and myself from this vicious attack?" Annie wondered. The woman's reflection showed an unusual black glow around her shape instead of the usual rainbow of colors that clung to the other shapes in the glass! It seemed to make the woman uglier. Weird! Annie looked at the librarian's hand resting on the table as she leaned into Maggie's face trying to scare Maggie even more. To Annie's horror she saw the image of a zorg tattooed on Mrs. Cain's hand!

"My Gosh!" cried Annie! "She has a zorg tattoo!" Annie's eyes were wide, staring at the woman's hand through her prism.

The librarian turned her attention back at Annie, eyes furious! They changed to a look of anger and then terror when she spotted the prism. She tried to grab the prism out of Annie's hand. Annie screamed, "Leave us alone! What do you think you are doing? I think you are an ugly witch! You are picking on us for no reason! We never touched any other books on that shelf, and we wouldn't have even looked at the book we did read if we knew it was off-limits. I know why you wanted to see me today. It was because of what I told you I had seen the last time I was here. You wanted to be sure we didn't investigate some more. You have a strange tattoo of the very creature I described to you! You lied to us! You knew exactly what I was talking about! I think you work for them!"

Mrs. Cain looked about to explode. She swung her arm at Annie again, trying to grab the prism from Annie's grasp. Annie yelled to the girls, "Look at her hand with your prisms!" Mrs. Cain spun towards Maggie and Michelle and saw the prisms they were holding. She was totally out of control by now. The clerk from behind the desk stood up and exclaimed, "What's going on?" Mrs. Cain turned towards the clerk, and then saw a handful of people watching. She straightened herself up, gave the girls a scathing look, and then walked up to the counter where her purse still rested. She took it and glaring again at the girls, left the library.

Annie was shaking and close to tears and the other girls weren't much better.

"Are you girls okay?" The clerk's hand rested on Annie's shoulder to calm her down. "What happened?"

"Mrs. Cain knows all about zorgs. Maybe she is a zorg! She's so mean. She's out to get us!" Annie said, shaking from all the adrenaline.

The clerk appeared bewildered. "I'm not sure what a zorg is, but since this incident involved a library employee, I have to file a report. Will you please wait while I call the library director?"

The girls stared at each other for a few minutes unable to think while the clerk walked back to her desk and used the phone.

The clerk returned. "Please follow me, girls." She led them down a short hall to an office. A pleasant-looking woman, perhaps in her late thirties, sat at a large desk.

"Good morning, girls. I'm Mrs. Susan Parks, the library director." She shook each girl's hand. "Let me see if I can find enough seats for you." She left the room for a minute and returned with two library chairs to add to the single chair that sat opposite the large brown office desk. "Please sit down. Natalie, would you mind bringing each of these girls a soda?" The clerk nodded with a smile, and left the room.

"I know it may seem odd for a librarian to serve students soda in a library," she noted with a smile. "Consider it a very special treat. Now, please tell me your names."

"I'm Maggie."

"Michelle."

"Annie."

The clerk sailed in noiselessly, placing an unopened can of cola before all four people seated around the desk. The sound of cans opening erupted in the silent room.

"So girls, I told Natalie to bring you girls back here because you were involved in a very vocal and almost violent incident with Mrs. Cain. Which of you can tell me exactly what happened?" Mrs. Parks' voice was very friendly, and her smile put Annie at ease.

"She definitely is *not* a zorg," Annie thought to herself. "I will start from the beginning," said Annie as she took a short sip of the fizzy cool liquid. Annie described the series of events beginning two days earlier including when her mom told her she had left her card at the library, and the reaction they got from Mrs. Cain when she returned to get it. "We were sitting around a table when Mrs. Cain came back. When she discovered we were waiting for her at the table, she walked over and accused Maggie and me of tearing two books in the Restricted Area on our last visit. She was intimidating us, trying to scare us, acting weird. I couldn't understand why she was so angry. While Mrs. Cain went on her rampage, I put my prism up to my eyes. Mrs. Cain had a black glow to her, and I saw a tattoo of a zorg on her left hand!"

Mrs. Parks studied Annie, trying to follow what the girl was saying. Annie explained. "I looked at her through the prism I have. All three of us have a prism. Just yesterday I met a lady who knew about the weird animal I saw by the roadside. We were trying to spot these very creatures on the way to the library today. Michelle's neighbor, Ms. Nichols, said these creatures have been around since the beginning of time and they are called zorgs. Ms. Nichols learned about them from her father when she was a child. He studied all types of interesting subjects. If it hadn't been for her, I wouldn't know anything about them. Do you happen to know her?"

Mrs. Parks replied, "No, I don't believe that I know Ms Nichols. She sounds very interesting! I am truly sorry for the incident two days ago with Mrs. Cain, and for the second episode she just put you through. I apologize on behalf of the library. Mrs. Cain has worked at this library ever since anyone can remember. It was her idea to restrict the use of the books in that section. Even so, I don't understand Mrs. Cain's actions today." She went on, "We try to go along with her, but she can be a bit difficult. Mrs. Cain was tenured many years ago, and it has been impossible to get her to leave. Her retirement is coming up, but with the complaint you girls have made this afternoon, it might be possible to submit a request that she take early retirement. I would hate to think that anyone would not encourage young people to use their library as often as possible. The library's purpose is to educate. If you want, you may go back now to the section where you were the other day, and take all the time you want to do research. I will use the materials I have at hand to help you in whatever way I can. I would like to keep what happened today quiet, though, for a little while, so I can try to find out more about the tattoo that you saw on Mrs. Cain's hand through the prism."

Mrs. Parks reached into her purse and took out a set of keys. She unlocked and opened the large drawer of her desk and removed a big prism. "We used to have several prisms here in this library, but they began to disappear. I kept this one under lock and key so that I, at least, would have one. Maybe their disappearance has something to do with Mrs. Cain and the tattoo you saw on her hand. I am very interested in these creatures of which you have spoken. Perhaps we can learn more from Mrs. Cain."

The girls stood up to leave and thanked Mrs. Parks. Annie asked Mrs. Parks to let them know if she found out any information about Mrs. Cain that might help them understand what was going on. The three girls gave her their home numbers and pointed out that they would be staying at Michelle's house for the next two days. She gave the girls her cell phone number if they discovered anything.

The trio went back to the section of the library where the Restricted Area was located. There were other spaces where books were missing, leaving gaping holes in the rows of books. Annie stood on a chair she dragged from the table for a closer view of the titles of some of the other books on the nearby shelf. She spotted C. S. Lewis's books referred to as the Space Trilogy. Out of the Silent Planet, Perelandra, and That Hideous Strength were three books Annie read two years ago. *Those books are excellent!* She thought. *Why had that woman placed them in this section? Other wonderful* books rested on the high bookshelves. What was this section used for?

The girls were ready to continue their search for the zorg. They wanted to go soon. Maggie ran to the desk and told the clerk to tell Mrs. Parks that the book they'd been reading was gone, the second they were accused of tearing, and others. The group left the library. They were anxious to continue their search for the zorg as originally planned.

The girls walked towards Michelle's house, past the same street where Annie had hurt herself. All three of them were looking through their prisms as they walked. Annie paused at the street where she'd seen the zorg run. They turned to go that way. The girls walked slowly, scanning the driveways, the bushes, and the basement doorways. Annie suddenly noticed a mailbox in front of one of the houses bearing the name 'Buanna Cain'. Annie stopped short. "Mrs. Cain's house!" she exclaimed, then quieted her voice. "Maybe this is where the zorg was heading that day."

The other girls exchanged anxious glances, and then followed Annie as she darted behind a big clunky car past Mrs. Cain's house in a neighbor's driveway. They peered back at the house they just passed.

It definitely needed some work. The dilapidated three story house had faded green paint, peeled and cracking. The yard was overgrown with bushes that needed pruning. The lawn was dry and almost dead. The yard looked creepy. Annie felt a chill go up her spine, though the temperature was almost ninety. "Let's get out of here. I don't like this place." Michelle and Maggie agreed. Just as they were about to leave, they heard a noise. Sure enough, it was Mrs. Cain!

The three girls crouched together tightly from behind the car, watching Mrs. Cain's every move. She walked from the backyard to the side porch, carrying a wooden box. Mrs. Cain put the box on the porch and unlatched the lid. She plunged her hand deep into her pocket and pulled out a set of keys on a ring. Tossing the keys into the box, she put the lid back down and fastened the latch with a pin.

The girls watched with keen interest as the woman pulled back a branch at the place where the porch intersected the house. There was an opening beneath the porch. She bent down and put the box under the porch. She let go of the branch and it swung back to hide the place. She walked to the backyard. A minute later she returned with an old coffee can. Once again, the mean-spirited librarian pulled back the bush and bent over to put the can under the porch. Mrs. Cain walked back to the backyard and out of sight. Before long they saw her emerge from the other side of the house, backing her old green Plymouth out of the driveway. The girls dove into a nearby hedge to avoid being seen. She rolled backwards into the street, put it into drive, and sped away.

The girls let out a sigh of relief. Once Mrs. Cain had gone they were more curious than ever. The girls felt that she was up to no good. What was in the box and the can? Why didn't she hide them in her house instead of out in the yard? Michelle nudged Annie, making her lose her train of thought.

"So, who's going to do it?" Michelle asked.

"Do what?" asked Annie.

"Duh," Michelle replied. "One of us has to find out what is under that porch. There is no way it will be me. Besides, I am the one having the sleepover. This will be one of my special privileges."

"Whatever!" Annie replied, suddenly scared of what might be under the porch. "If anything, we should all go together, for protection."

"You guys are such weenies!" Maggie exclaimed. "I'll do it. But I also want you guys to know that you will owe me a burger and fries the next time we're at the Snack Shop. Maybe even a chocolate shake."

Annie and Michelle nodded in agreement, though Annie wasn't quite ready to spend her ten-dollar bill her dad gave her. As the girls carefully studied their surroundings to be sure Maggie would be safe, Annie noticed a trail. "It looks like there is a path to that opening under the porch." They could see a worn line on the dry lawn leading from a tree in the front yard to the bush. "Why is there a path leading from that tree? Do you think it could have been made by zorgs?"

"Ms. Nichols said the zorgs are in a slightly different dimension," Maggie replied. "Could their paws on this dimension make a path?" Maggie quickly tiptoed to the open spot by the porch, scrunched her body between the porch and the disguising branch and dropped down on all fours. She crawled a distance under the structure, then sat to examine the contents of the coffee can and box. Annie and Michelle could barely see Maggie's shape through the lattice work, but she called to them in a loud whisper, "The can is full of prisms-maybe from the library. I'll see what's in the box!"

It seemed to be taking Maggie a long time. Annie anxiously pulled the prism from her top pocket and put it up to her eye. "Oh, my gosh!" she silently screamed. There before her was the form of a zorg advancing on the path. Its shape was not like the other objects reflected through the glass. Instead of having a rainbow-colored shimmer about its silhouette, it was surrounded by black, just like Mrs. Cain! The zorg headed towards the porch. Annie guessed that the zorg was able to make a path, after all, and it seemed to know exactly where it was going as it headed towards the porch! A beautiful butterfly fluttered through the air above the zorg, lilting through the summer sky. The zorg noticed it, and with a swift movement, grabbed the fragile butterfly, snapped the wings off its body and ate them. Annie could faintly smell the fowl creature, about twenty feet away. She touched Michelle's shoulder and motioned for her to look at the zorg. Michelle drew her prism to her eyes and Annie heard her gasp. Looking at each other, the girls now worried about Maggie, still under the porch with the zorg quickly approaching. "What should we do?" mouthed Annie to Michelle, very concerned. They crossed their fingers and began silently saying the Lord's Prayer as they watched the evil creature. Slobbering as he finished up the butterfly, he flinched suddenly, like he was having a spasm, and moved towards the porch. It disappeared from view, behind the lattice, only inches from Maggie!

Michelle grasped Annie's hand and squeezed it. She whispered, "We've got to help Maggie!" Annie nodded yes, and they both stood up. Just then the prism Annie was peering through showed the zorg emerge from the porch, carrying the keys! "Thank goodness, the zorg left Maggie alone!" Annie looked at the scene without the glass prism, and could barely see the keys with her naked eye. "When a zorg holds onto something from this dimension, it must slightly disappear," she thought. She watched as the keys headed towards the back of the house. Annie put the prism back to her eyes and saw the zorg scamper around the corner into the backyard, its barbed tail the last thing to disappear from sight.

They waited for a minute or so, then quietly moved into Mrs. Cain's yard. Annie crept to the corner of the house where the zorg had gone, and saw an old single car garage with the door open, and beside it, a brick shed. The door to the shed was ajar, and the set of keys dangled from the lock. There was a single window with four filthy panes. Through the dirty window Annie could see a thin light streaming from a hanging light bulb. She looked around the rest of the yard. Branches and rubbish had accumulated for years. The dead lawn was sparse under the straggly trees that had somehow managed to stay alive without care. There was no other sign of zorgs besides the one in the shed. She tiptoed back to the porch.

Maggie was emerging from where she had been hidden. Annie told her, "The zorg is in the shed in the backyard!" Michelle held the branch while Maggie stood up and stretched her back. Maggie said in whispered tones, "What a close call! When I got there, I looked in the box and saw the books and keys, and then in the can where I found prisms! I was checking out one of the biggest prisms from the coffee can when my guardian angel must have prompted me to look through it towards where you were waiting. I saw you both looking through your prisms at the side yard where that ugly thing was tearing apart that poor butterfly and eating it."

"My knees were shaking as I scooted back as far under the porch as I could. I held my breath when it came under the porch. I watched it as it took the keys from the box, and then it left. It didn't see me, thank God. When its stink reached my nose I thought I would throw up. I prayed as hard as I have ever prayed in my life!" Maggie whispered. She reached down and lugged the box out first and set it up on the porch. She unlatched the lid.

"Look at the top book!" Annie exclaimed. It's the missing book from the library!" Maggie took the big book out of the box. Beneath it were more books. Annie took one book and read the title on its spine. It was a Holy Bible. She opened the cover to the front inside flap. There was the property label of the library! She took another book from the box and opened it. She checked the remaining books in the crate. All of them were Holy Bibles, and they all came from the library.

"What's going on?" Annie looked at her friends, her face expressing the weirdness of the situation. What motive was driving that strange lady? Annie's expression asked the question that none of the girls could answer-why these books were stolen from the library?

"We need to get this stuff and get out of here. That zorg is around!" Annie reminded the others. Maggie reached under the porch and retrieved the rusty three-pound coffee can with a tin lid. It was filled with prisms.

Maggie said, "Let's take the box to show Ms. Nichols. I want to know why Mrs. Cain didn't want us to use this book."

Annie agreed. "That's a good idea. Besides, Mrs. Cain might try to take them again from the library if we take them back there right now. We need to keep them somewhere safe."

Annie motioned for the girls to be very quiet. She tiptoed to the backyard again. The other girls followed. Annie pressed close to the house as she approached the corner, and leaned her head around the corner to see the backyard, using her prism. The yard was still clear! She dropped the prism from her eyes to scout the area. The thin light shone through the filthy glass. The door to the shed was still open with the set of keys hanging from the lock!

Annie watched for a second longer and then backed around the corner again. "The zorg is still in the shed!" Her two friends each took a turn peeking around the corner to see for themselves. Annie whispered, "Should I lock the door to the shed and grab the keys?" Michelle and Maggie looked at her and then at each other.

"After the close call I had just awhile ago?" Maggie exclaimed in a low whisper. "Let's just get out of here!"

The girls retraced their steps to the porch to retrieve the can and wooden container. Maggie and Annie picked up the crate, and each one taking a handle, they carried it together. Michelle gripped the can full of prisms, and pressed the lid tight. All three adventurers crept back through the split in the overgrown hedge that surrounded Mrs. Cain's house. Once they reached the street they walked as fast as they could all the way back to Michelle's house.

Michelle opened her front door and the girls went directly to the kitchen. They got a drink of water first, and then collapsed around the breakfast nook, still panting from all of the exertion. Lingering a minute more in the cool air-conditioned kitchen, Maggie started to joke at how fast they could get to Michelle's from Mrs. Cain's house. The red-faced girls laughed. Michelle noticed the note that was left on the table by her mom. It said that her parents would be back soon. They had gone shopping for a few things for the trip. The three girls finished their water, and then went next door to Ms. Nichols' house.

Ms. Nichols looked out to see the three sweating girls holding their treasure, excitement in their eyes. She opened the door. Maggie and Annie lugged the box in, and Michelle carried the coffee can. Ms. Nichols exclaimed, "What is all of this?"

Maggie said, "You won't believe what happened this morning!" The two girls set the box on the floor in one motion, and Annie lifted the lid. Ms. Nichols' eyes opened wide when she saw the old book on top.

Michelle put the can down on the folded newspaper on the table. All three girls started talking at once, then laughed, realizing that no one could hear anyone talk. They took turns describing the events starting at the library and leading up to the discovery of the items they had retrieved, including the fact that the books they found were taken from the library!

"What a coincidence that you found Mrs. Cain's house on the way home!" Ms. Nichols exclaimed. She picked up the old book and began paging through it. The sound of voices drifted in from the next room. It sounded like two people talking.

"Is someone else here?" Maggie asked.

Michelle laughed. "No, those are Ms. Nichols' parrots. I used to come over and talk to them. They have a cage in the corner of the kitchen."

"Michelle, please show the girls the parrots," said Ms. Nichols absent-mindedly as she lifted the book out of the box and began to look through it. "I would like to read through this book for a minute." Annie and Maggie followed Michelle to the kitchen.

The parrots chattered to each other from their perches, and then one of them said, "Ugly zorgs, ugly zorgs, bringing misery to the hoards!" Ms. Nichols could hear the birds easily, from the chair where she was examining the book in the next room.

"I've never heard them say that before! I know they do have long memories. Perhaps one of them heard about zorgs from my father. He gave me these birds. Or maybe they've had an experience with zorgs. I never heard my father say anything like that."

There was a knock at the door. Ms. Nichols answered it. Michelle's mom stood there. "Hi, Gussie," she said. "Could I please speak with the girls? We're about to leave on our trip and I wanted to go over a few things with them before we go. They can come right back over."

"Sure, Jeannie. That would be just fine! Enjoy your trip!"

"Thanks, Gussie. I appreciate you keeping an eye on the girls this weekend. Thank you, again!"

The girls followed Michelle's mom next door. She gave her daughter a list of everything she wanted her to do while they were away. The girls promised to go to bed at ten and not to eat too much junk food. Michelle's parents had brought back a bucket of chicken and mashed potatoes, biscuits and gravy and a container of coleslaw for them to have for dinner. Her dad came from the bedroom with the two suitcases. He set them on the living room rug and took out his wallet.

"Hey, honey, here is some money for pizza. You girls have some fun." He smiled at his daughter and gave her a couple of bills.

"Girls, help yourselves to the food in the fridge!" added Michelle's mom as she went to hug her daughter before they left. "I bought lots of cold cuts for sandwiches!" Michelle walked her parents out to the car and gave them another hug before they drove away. The girls were on their own!

They returned to Ms. Nichols' house, bringing dinner with them. She led them to the kitchen and laid out the table with silverware, napkins and plates. Michelle got iced-tea and milk from the refrigerator and set the containers in the center of the table. Ms. Nichols went back to the refrigerator to get celery and carrot sticks. She found a container of ranch dip to go with it. No one even realized how hungry they were until they started to eat. The meal was perfect!

Even the parrots went to their respective trays and ate their meal while the people ate at the table. Annie and Maggie giggled at the birds antics. All three girls recounted details from their afternoon adventure while they finished eating. The girls threw away the trash and put the extra leftovers in Ms. Nichols' fridge. Tiggy meowed at the back door. Tiggy could smell the chicken dinner from outside! Ms. Nichols put some tasty morsels into Tiggy's bowl, and he was happily eating lunch when the group returned to the den containing the loot from the afternoon's adventure.

Ms. Nichols opened the old book again, and continued from where she left off. "I searched this book for the damage that Mrs. Cain said you had done while to it while you were next door with Michelle's parents. So far I can see none."

"She just made that up!" Annie replied.

Ms. Nichols opened the book and found the section about Noah's Ark. She read the explanation of the rainbow, and said, "How interesting! The rainbow wasn't possible until droplets of water in mist or rain could be penetrated by direct sunlight. No wonder God promised never to destroy the earth again by water. It would be impossible to duplicate that volume of flood water without the melting shield. This illustration is so interesting!" she said, as the girls watched, listened and learned.

Ms. Nichols turned to the beginning of the book. She systematically paged through its entirety, looking for anything that might be helpful to understanding why Mrs. Cain had removed this book from the girl's reach. Ms. Nichols remarked as she searched the volume, "Something in this book made Buanna nervous, I believe." Towards the back of the book, she came upon a chapter with an illustration. There stood a zorg, mixing up a potion, in a spider web-ridden laboratory. In the distance, smoke and the ruins of buildings were visible through the open laboratory window. Silhouettes of men pushing wheelbarrows filled with corpses reflected the depths of misery. Burn piles in the remote background smoldered with burning, plague-infested victims. Rats roamed everywhere.

"This must be an illustration representing the bubonic plague-a bacterium that killed millions of people in China and Europe during the fourteenth century. My dad actually did some historical research on this pandemic-fleas living on the blood of infected rats spread the bacteria. The bacteria lives on in small animals and rodents, so even in our age of modern medicine and sanitation, people will continue to contract it, though not with the mortality rate as in centuries past. It's quite obvious that these creatures are not our friends."

As if to follow Ms. Nichols cue, she started reading, *"Zorgs are known as the Devil's helpers. They have worked hand in hand with Lucifer since the division between good and evil at the dawn of time. Once beautiful harp players, Zorgs followed Satan's rebellious path, and wanted a big slice of the action. Satan was more than happy to oblige. Found beyond the gates of the Garden of Eden in large numbers, they were always prevented by God's own angels from ever setting foot there.*

"Adam and Eve's fall from grace began the saga of "God's Project" on this earth. Raising up a people to serve Him, and be His own, out of this bloodline He begot a Son, Jesus Christ, God made Man, to take on the sins of the world, and to overcome death, which was the result of sin on earth.

"There has always been a spiritual point to life on the planet earth. People have always had to make one of two choices. There is no middle ground. We may choose not to think about it, but people must either serve Good or Evil. Each of us knows who we serve.

"During the end times, the zorgs, the devils, and Lucifer will increasingly persecute humanity, so that through those very hard times, people will give up hope and turn away from God and His promises. It will appear that wickedness has won the day until at the very end when God Incarnate, Jesus Christ, will come back in His second coming. He will slay the Antichrist with his breath, since he has already won the battle over death

through His own death and resurrection. Then will come the judgment of the living and the dead.

"The Zorgs play an important role in this persecution. Zorgs, though they live in a dimension invisible to the naked eye, can still physically manipulate earthly objects. They might find some water to make that ice patch a little bigger so that someone slips and falls. They use their dark aura to make everyone's face look a little meaner during intense conversations. They distract you by pinching your baby so you forget to lock your door-and then they rob your house. They drag contaminated kerchiefs from house to house, infecting the inhabitants during the sick season. They instill doubt and confusion whenever possible.

"But perhaps the thing they do best is their ability to increase one's selfishness. This aspect of their mission is the most confusing because it is not known how they do it. The more selfish a civilization becomes, however, the easier the societal and governmental infrastructure can break down. The farther from God the society, the quicker the zorgs can bring the society to its knees, but unfortunately not in prayer, which would have prevented the zorg population explosion that continues to destabilize all communities. Zorgs love pain, suffering, and sadness. They derive pleasure and energy from people's unhappiness."

A chill ran down Annie's back. "That makes me shiver."

Ms. Nichols smiled at the girl reassuringly and continued, *"Cats can smell zorgs and kill them, but usually humans would never know when this occurs, since the zorg is invisible to the human eye. It is believed that a prism on a cat's collar allows the cat to see the zorgs clearly."*

Annie asked Ms. Nichols if she thought that her cat would be a good zorger, like a mouser, if she fixed him up with a prism collar. Mrs. Nichols laughed.

"I don't know how ferocious a cat has to be, but my little Tiggy is pretty mild mannered. He doesn't try to hurt my parrots, in fact they are all good friends! It's funny to watch the parrots pick off his fleas once on awhile. They call him Pretty Kitty. But I must say, I have never seen a mouse around my house. He may very well be a good mouser and a zorger!" The girls laughed.

They returned their attention to the book Ms. Nichols was reading. When she finished the article, the girls decided to call Mrs. Parks' cell phone and let her know what had happened since they left the library that morning.

"Hello?" Mrs. Parks answered.

"Hi! This is Annie! You won't believe what happened after we saw you today! When we left the library this afternoon, we found Mrs. Cain's house. While we were looking at her place from the street, she came into the side yard near where we were hiding. We watched her put something under her porch. After she left, we looked. She had stashed some books taken from the library, including the one we were looking at on Wednesday when she got so mad at us! Also, she hid a large coffee can filled with prisms!"

Mrs. Parks was astonished. "After you girls left, Mrs. Cain came back to the library. She wanted me to revoke your library privileges for violating library policies. Though the three of you violated a library rule, I told her that before taking disciplinary action, I recommended evaluating with our library board the current library policies to see if they need revision. It's late now, but maybe I can call you or you can come to the library tomorrow if I find out anything else. Talk to you tomorrow."

Ms. Nichols took one of the Holy Bibles from the crate, now resting on the floor of the den. After looking at the label inside, she flipped through the Bible.

"Why do you think Buanna Cain took these books from the library?" She looked at the visitors with a questioning look.

Michelle responded, "Probably just to keep people from reading them!"

Ms. Nichols grinned, "Why didn't I think of that? But then, just like the zorgs, no amount of trying can hide God's word and authority!"

The girls sat cross-legged on the rug by Ms. Nichols' chair, while she read many interesting things from the book. Michelle got up and made hot tea seasoned with cinnamon sticks and a little honey, and brought everyone a cup. They sipped their tea and spent a couple of hours mulling things over.

At about six that evening, Ms. Nichols went to the kitchen and heated up the leftover mashed potatoes, gravy and biscuits. The three girls played with the cat and stretched their legs a bit before Ms. Nichols called them in to eat. Annie finished her second helping of mashed potatoes and her piece of chicken.

"Today was so fun!" she said. "Except I couldn't believe it when we saw that zorg. That was scary!"

Maggie grinned. "This is an adventure we will always remember!"

Once again the girls helped Ms. Nichols with the clean-up from the late afternoon meal. They lingered awhile longer, but began to feel tired from the long day. The girls decided they would go back to Michelle's to watch some television.

"Maybe there's a good movie on tonight!" Michelle said.

"I believe I will stay up a bit longer and read through the book some more." Ms. Nichols said goodnight to them as they headed back next door, their prisms in hand.

Saturday, 7:03 a.m.

Annie awoke first. She glanced at the clock on the wall-a couple minutes after seven. Michelle and Maggie were still dead to the world in their sleeping bags on the floor. It was unusual for her to get up so early on a Saturday morning, but she couldn't sleep another minute. She went to the kitchen and made herself a bowl of cereal. The bowls, spoons and cereal boxes were neatly situated on the kitchen counter top. She was on a second bowl of Wheaties, re-reading everything on the box, when the telephone's shrill ring broke the silence. Annie answered it and identified herself. It was Mrs. Parks from the library.

"Hi, Annie. I'm sure this is a little early to be calling you after you girls probably stayed up late, but I wanted to tell you about the strange events of last night-"

"-Wait! Can we call you back from Ms. Nichols house? Since she is helping us, we could go right over and call you from there." Annie hung up and woke up the other two, shaking with excitement. This could be another very interesting day!

Within minutes the three girls stood at Ms. Nichols' front door. She answered in her night robe and a cup of coffee in her right hand. "Mrs. Parks called just a minute ago," said Michelle. "Annie told her we would call her right back from your house." Ms. Nichols ushered them into the den, brought the telephone closer to Annie, and sat beside her at the table. Annie punched in the number.

"Annie?" Mrs. Parks answered.

Annie responded. "We are all here at Ms. Nichols calling you back on speaker phone, O.K.?"

"Yes, that's great!" Mrs. Parks continued, "I am pleased to meet you by phone, Ms. Nichols."

Ms. Nichols replied, "The pleasure is mine, Mrs. Parks. Please call me Augusta, or Gussie."

Mrs. Parks said, "Thank you, Augusta. You can call me Susan. Thank you so much for getting involved. Frankly, this whole thing came as a bolt out of the blue, and I am glad to have you available to help me understand exactly what is going on! It has been a very long night and it all has to do with Mrs. Cain. Yesterday after you girls left, Mrs. Cain came back to the library in one of her worst moods ever. I called her into my office and asked her about the commotion with you girls at the library that afternoon. She exploded into a black temper. She said that children shouldn't even be allowed in a library. I said to her, "Libraries exist to educate and no one should work here if they don't accept that as a reality." She was so angry with me she was ready to spit."

Mrs. Parks continued. "I was hired as Director more than a dozen years ago. The board told me she had applied for the same position, but they wouldn't consider her because although she knew the library inside and out, she often had conflicts with the library staff. She did not like people very much. I found out from the previous library director that Mrs. Cain was hired as a teenager and was married briefly to a man who was found guilty of a felony many years ago. He died in prison. That is all I know about her. I don't know of any friends or family that she keeps in contact with. The library has been her whole life, sad as that sounds. I asked her if she would explain why she had treated you girls in such an accusatory manner. I explained that your parents might make a complaint against the library. Mrs. Cain said I was being overprotective of the three of you and that severe disciplinary action was required. That is when I told her that I thought she should consider retirement, because her emotions were interfering with her work. Mrs. Cain stormed out of my office right then, went to her desk, took some items and walked out the door. As she left, she stopped by my office and said she hated the way the world was going and she quit!"

"I never even thought to ask her for her key. I hoped that was the end of her. Then last night around midnight the police called and asked me to meet them in the library parking lot. They wanted me to open up the library. When I got there, they told me they had spotted a light inside at about eleven thirty. I unlocked the door and we all went in but couldn't see or hear anything unusual. While we toured the rows of books, I noticed a shaft of light down a side aisle. The police investigated and found that the whole bookshelf against the inside wall was on a swivel. We pushed it open to find a secret, well-lit room full of boxes of papers and other old furniture like desks and chairs. I was so surprised! There stood Mrs. Cain with her back to us! She was so preoccupied she must not have heard us. She spun around at the sound, and when she saw me she ran at me and tried to knock me down. The officers grabbed her and held her with handcuffs. I looked around the area where she stood and saw a diagram of pipes and a list of illnesses, such as malaria, tuberculosis, and the bubonic plague. A chill went down my spine.

"The police officers began searching the large room. I thought about what you girls said about the tattoo on Mrs. Cain's hand. I ran to my office to get my prism. Mrs. Cain shrieked when she saw it! I held it up and looked at the tattoo you described on her hand, and then I looked around the rest of the room. Crouching in the corners were more than a dozen of the same shaped creatures as shown on her tattoo! I told the officers that we were not alone, and had them look at the zorgs, too. The officers drew their guns. The zorgs scattered, looking for hiding places. The police took Mrs. Cain into custody, and the room was sealed off in an attempt to keep the creatures from escaping. We don't know if the door will stop them, but we hope so. I think the police got a search warrant for her home, also.

"Neither the police nor I have a clue about what we are dealing with," Mrs. Parks added. "Would you mind if I call the Chief of Police now to ask him if it would be possible to have you come to the library when they do their investigation? The four of you have much more information about this. I'd be happy to pick you up." Ms. Nichols and the girls agreed.

After they hung up, Ms. Nichols said, "Girls, let's see what we have in the tin can. She opened the lid and one by one, she put the prisms on the tabletop. Some were even larger than the one Mrs. Parks showed the girls from her locked desk at the library the day before. After Augusta took out the last large prism, she saw an object at the bottom of the can.

She dumped it into her open palm. It was an ancient collar with a tiny prism attached. Ms. Nichols exclaimed, "It is exactly like the collar on the cat in the illustration we saw in my father's old book!" The leather was curled up, and the stitching frayed. Ms. Nichols carefully opened up the buckle and held the collar up for a closer inspection. Inside the collar was a faint inscription that read: "For Jasper, My Beloved Cat." Beneath these words was the date: "1629." Ms. Nichols held it gingerly. The girls smiled at the dinky little collar with a dangling, tiny prism.

Ms. Nichols left the room for a few minutes. The girls inspected the tiny prism collar laying curled up on the table. Soon Ms. Nichols returned with a new cat collar with a place for tags. It was red leather with little rhinestones all the way around it.

"I will put that prism onto this collar. We'll save the other collar. It is so old! It probably belongs in a museum." Ms. Nichols carefully removed the prism from the old collar and put it on the new collar. She picked up Tiggy and put him on her lap. She placed the collar around his neck. He started purring from his master's attention. Everyone giggled when Tiggy batted at the new dangling object bumping his chest. Ms. Nichols scratched him behind the ears and he began purring even louder. "Tiggy is the best!" Augusta smiled, as the content animal stretched out on her lap, watching the girls.

The phone rang. It was Mrs. Parks calling back to say she had spoken to Chief of Police Graham and he asked Mrs. Parks to arrange a meeting at the library. Mrs. Parks said she'd pick them up in an hour or so if that would work with their schedule. Ms. Nichols agreed and placed the phone back on the cradle after they made the plans.

The old book lay beside the empty coffee can and the dozen or more prisms arranged on the table. Ms. Nichols picked up the still purring cat and set him gently to the floor near the wooden crate that still held the several Bibles stolen from the library. She opened the book and paged through it. She had taken time to mark some places in the book. She turned to the first bookmark and began reading.

"The zorgs have few natural enemies. Some zorgs are hundreds of years old. Zorgs weaken with age, but can regain a certain amount of vitality from the pain and suffering of people. A person in pain or sorrow emits a type of energy. This energy, or 'prana', recharges a zorg and gives him renewed strength. A zorg obtains the energy by breathing the air near the person that is suffering. Since zorgs are invisible to the naked eye, the person is not aware of what is happening when the zorg himself actually inflicts the pain."

Annie thought about the afternoon her bike chain came off. "Do you think it is possible that a zorg caused the problem I had with my bike chain somehow?"

Ms. Nichols smiled. "If that did happen, the action backfired on the zorg, because now people are after them!" She continued where she left off. *"From the earliest of times, God has instructed mankind through His Word. Mankind must take this command seriously. Through the Word comes the knowledge of the futility of evil, but more importantly, the grace through faith that is needed to discipline our conscience and serve God, not Satan."*

"If you take the word 'LIVE' and hold it up to the mirror, the word 'EVIL' is reflected, the opposite meaning. It is an odd fact that the correct spiritual response is often exactly opposite to the natural response of the world. Jesus told us to love our enemies, and to turn the other cheek when sinned against. We are supposed to consciously choose to act as a shock absorber and show kindness to our enemies. 'Vengeance is mine, sayeth the Lord.'

"We all will be called to account for our deeds on this Earth. The reward for doing these selfless acts will be repaid tenfold, but in God's time, in God's manner. This 'Coin of the Heavenly Realm' is kept safe where no burglar can steal it. Our bodies are the physical tools that God created to bring Him glory," read Augusta. *"We are the Body of Christ, all called to perform a different function. We are God's hands and feet.*

"Accepting Christ's sacrifice for our sins and living for His glory does not mean that life will be easy. Faith that goes unchallenged will remain unchanged. Pain and suffering have the power to transform a person's life. The Christian who is suffering must respond by consciously offering their pain and suffering to God, to be used according to His good will, to bring others to Him, rather than thrashing out at God or others for their problems or pain. This conscious act, just like prayer, is a strong defense in the spiritual battle constantly raging on earth.

"When prayers and spiritual sacrifices to God diminish, it is as though a darkness and weakness descends on the earth. When zorgs tempt a human to sin, or cause pain and suffering, if the human victims respond by praying and offering up the pain to God, the damage backfires on the zorgs.

"It is said that by continuously and earnestly praying the Lord's Prayer during an assault, the energy will be reversed, and will turn the curse back onto the offending zorg. A close relationship to God and constant prayers of the faithful are considered the best methods to curb the damage caused by the zorgs' focused mission to destroy our planet.

"Zorgs delight in thwarting men's efforts to avoid evil and to seek the Truth. With every assault against mankind's accomplishments, against men's faith in God, they prolong humanity's efforts to find the Truth. Everyone knows that when the battle is over, good will prevail. It is written throughout the Holy Bible.

"God saw the helpless position of the man overcome with evil, and knew that they would not be strong enough to fight the zorgs alone. God therefore decreed that the elves would have dominion over the evil zorgs. This battle has been raging since the fall of man. Zorgs are an abomination to God Almighty, since they derive great pleasure in mankind's failure to glorify, fear, and honor Him."

Mrs. Nichols read on, "Not all humans are the enemies of zorgs. People are subject to the spirit which they seek. Evil people help the zorg movement even when they are unaware of any zorg movement or evil force. Simply by not seeking God and reading the Holy Bible, people give the zorgs the opportunity for assault. When trial and tribulation come, these hopeless souls weaken physically and emotionally as their energy drains from their body and mind into the zorg. The plan laid out by Satan is simple. Divide and conquer. Separate people from the knowledge and love of God, and evil will hold them.

"There is also a type of human knowingly in league with these creatures. They are called humanz. The people that help the zorgs can be identified by a telltale sign on their hand easily visible to zorgs, animals, and elves. Tattoos are placed on humans' hand by the zorgs. Often, if a zorg is able to claim one family member, the pain and hurt caused by that family member often lures the entire family to the evil side.

"The humanz involved with zorgs are most despicable. They choose to serve evil rather than serving good. They are power-hungry, and refuse to find success in life through the normal channels of hard work and study. They instead use manipulation and pain to grow in power. Their outlook on life is mean-spirited. The only power they will ever achieve is through their association with the zorgs. Zorgs help place these human comrades in valuable positions to support their cause."

Ms. Nichols turned to the next page. Her face brightened a bit. "There seems to be a silver lining to this dark, dark cloud." The girls could only half-smile. On the left side of the page was a formula for an antidote.

"Sometime ago it was discovered that the zorg population is allergic to the following recipe. The directions read:

ZORG POISON
ANTIDOTE TO THE VERMIN PEST

Using elements found on the earth,
Mix one ounce of moss
With a quart of living water
Stir in one tablespoon of salt
Place the mixture in direct sunlight
Then place a prism into the glass container
So that the sunlight can pass through the prism
Allow the solution to sit in the sunlight for one hour

Ms. Nichols said, "After we meet with Mrs. Parks and the Chief of Police at the library, we should collect some moss! My family farm is just north of town. There is a lovely old wooded area out there. It is a beautiful place. We could go there to collect moss for this antidote. Today is a great day to go for a visit. It will be fun!"

Michelle, Maggie and Annie couldn't agree more. Augusta continued reading specific items from the places she had marked.

"A prism is another of the zorgs' most dreaded objects, because zorgs feel a vacuum or void of energy in the presence of prisms. Prisms were made to separate rays of light, and since a zorg is made of the darkness, a prism makes the zorg feel a pain similar to the ache of a dry socket when one has had a tooth removed and it doesn't heal correctly. In order to prevent pain to a zorg, zorgs keep prisms buried or in sealed containers."

The doorbell rang. Ms. Nichols answered the door. There stood the Library Director. Mrs. Parks introduced herself and Ms. Nichols asked her to come in. The girls greeted her.

"I am here a little early," Mrs. Parks noted. "I was interested in seeing what you girls found at Mrs. Cain's home." Annie showed Mrs. Parks the books they had found. She joined them around the cozy room and Ms. Nichols re-read some of the more important paragraphs that they had read earlier. She had a few more pages to finish reading to the girls that she completed while Mrs. Parks listened in.

After she read the last part she stood up. Turning to Mrs. Parks, she said, "We will bring this book along when we go to meet with the police at the library! This information will help the officers to better understand this threat. We'll also bring the can of prisms! Anyone helping with this problem will need one!" Mrs. Parks gladly agreed.

Maggie added, "Our uncle sells eyeglasses. He has plain demonstration glasses on display for customers when they select their new glasses. Maybe we could each get a pair of demo frames and mount the prisms on them, so we don't always have to hold the prism up to our eyes!"

"It's worth a try," said Mrs. Parks. Maggie made the call, and her uncle answered the phone. At Maggie's request he told her he had several extra frames that had gone out of style, so anytime they wanted, they could come by and pick some out. He was planning to be there all day, and he wasn't too busy to help them.

Mrs. Parks borrowed the phone and dialed the police department. Chief of Police John Graham answered. Mrs. Parks finalized the meeting time and hung up. He and the detective unit would arrive at the library at about one o'clock or so.

Ms. Nichols went to the basement to get a roll of thin copper wire, thinking it would be useful for attaching the prisms. She placed the wire and a pair of needle-nosed pliers into a canvas bag, along with the prisms that were on the table. Michelle carried the bag out to the car for Ms. Nichols. Maggie and Annie once again lugged the books.

The optometrist office wasn't far. When they arrived, Maggie and Michelle's Uncle Vince showed them a display case full of obsolete sample frames in the storage room. They were given their choice of frames on which to fasten the prisms. The kind elderly man asked Michelle and Maggie what they and their friends were going to do with the glasses.

Ms. Nichols chimed in. "We plan to experiment. We want to see whether we can mount the prisms onto the frames so we can see through the prisms right side up." He laughed at her reply and said they would all look like space people wearing a prism on their glasses, but he offered to help them try to figure it out.

He used his equipment to drill holes in the frames, and then attached the prisms with the copper wire. He found a way to lift each prism slightly when mounting them to make the view right side up. The glasses looked weird, and they were kind of heavy, but they would work. Ms. Nichols handed him about ten prisms from the bag. He fastened every one of them to a pair of frames. Vince gave Ms. Nichols a separate bag of display glasses for her to make more of the glasses, if they wanted more later. The group thanked him and left.

Mrs. Parks treated everyone to lunch at Goodie's Grill. They were able to discuss more of what had been learned about the zorgs. Mrs. Parks ordered a burger and fries to go, which she would drop off for Vince at the eyeglass company before they went to the meeting at the library. She wanted to express her appreciation for all of his hard work that morning.

A few minutes before one o'clock, the talkative crew arrived at the library. Ms. Nichols was the first one out of the car. She held up a prism to her eyes and scanned the parking lot. "I thought it would be good to make sure none of the creatures were lurking around." She smiled. Shortly after, the patrol car pulled into the library parking lot. Mrs. Parks walked over to the Chief, shook his hand and introduced Ms. Nichols and the girls.

The Library Director walked to the back of her car and unlocked the trunk. Ms. Nichols helped Annie and Maggie lift out the crate of books, placing them beside the car. Annie and Maggie explained how they watched Mrs. Cain hide these things beneath her porch. Ms. Nichols lifted the top book to reveal the various Bibles that had been secreted away from the library that all but filled the box. She then identified the ancient book containing so much useful information regarding zorgs. She carried the book to the front of the car and placed it on the hood. Opening the old book to the page containing the Zorg Antidote, she held the place while the Chief leaned over the hood and read the ingredients of the remedy. He bent down and reached into the wooden crate beside him and removed one of the library copies of the Holy Bible. "I suppose trying to prevent the public access to Holy Scripture is the only motive I can think of, right now, for Buanna Cain to have taken these Bibles home."

Mrs. Parks added, "Ms. Nichols is the one that told the girls about the zorgs. She knew they were visible through a prism. That was how last night I knew to use the prism I kept in my office to spot the zorgs in that room." Turning to Ms. Nichols, she added, "Thank you for any help you are willing to give us. Frankly, I feel like I am living in a fiction novel. I never imagined such things could be real!"

Ms. Nichols blushed slightly and smiled. "No problem. I'm pleased to be of help. The stories I heard about them as a child had all but faded in my mind. Then, coincidently, just the other day I'd brought an old box of my father's books back from the family farm north of town. I had just been going through the old volumes when I came upon a short article with an illustration describing zorgs as creatures discovered by Galileo. The discovery was made when he had so many other things bothering him in his life. Strange circumstances prevented the zorgs from becoming well-known. It was fascinating reading."

"It was only a few days later that my neighbor, Michelle, brought her friends over to talk to me about a creature one of the girls had seen. Annie's drawings really got my attention. She had drawn a zorg! My eyes couldn't believe it. Of course, I went upstairs to get the book. It didn't have much more in it regarding the invisible beasts, but it was enough to explain the thing Annie had seen with her teary eyes in a reflection! These girls are the best! They have wonderful spirits and enthusiasm for life and truth. It was their adventurous side (and Annie's misfortune, I might add) that helped uncover this unsettling situation."

Augusta picked up the bag of prism-glasses. "This morning these girls got these glasses made for us. There are several sets for you and your men. We each have a pair."

The Chief took the container of prism glasses, curiously tried on a pair himself, and then asked his aide to distribute a pair to each of the officers. Chief Graham addressed the group, "Until we understand what is happening, the best policy would be to keep this quiet from the general public. We don't even know what we are dealing with."

The chief motioned for his deputy to move the crate of Bibles into the chief's cruiser. "We will have to label this as evidence," he noted. He directed an officer to stand position at the Library door. "Be sure to keep these glasses on. You need to know when a zorg is nearby!" To another officer he said, "Post a notice on the library's entrance. Simply say that the library will be closed until further notice."

Mrs. Parks unlocked the front door of the library. John Graham and his men went in first, strong flashlights in hand, to make sure no creatures lurked in ambush. The group waited at the door until a cop returned with his new, clunky headgear, and gave them the 'all clear'. With everyone wearing their glasses, it was a strange looking group. Mrs. Parks led her visitors to a table where they put the book and other items they'd brought along.

The police officers quickly explored and secured the main rooms of the library. The Chief then directed an officer to open the door of the secret wall of books to expose the hidden room. The officer flipped a light switch on the inner wall. Incandescent light filled the area. The officers systematically entered and searched the hidden room but the zorgs were gone! Chief Graham secretly sighed with relief. He still wasn't prepared to try to apprehend, much less arrest a creature naked to the human eye.

"There must be a means of escape, other than the panel wall that the officers sealed off last night," the Chief remarked. The officers searched through the room's cupboards and shelves. Annie and the girls followed Mrs. Parks' lead and began looking for zorgs under tables and on the floor on their hands and knees. They peered below desks and around boxes, to be sure that the vermin weren't hiding right under their noses. With the aid of their new glasses, they were sure that there were no creatures in that room.

Michelle exclaimed, "Ouch! There is something bulging under the rug right here. It hurt my knee!" The others gathered to pull back the rug to see what caused the uneven surface. There was a trap door! The policeman nearest the girls asked them to stand back while he and his partner checked it out. He pulled on the ring in the center of the square metal door and it easily lifted open. A flashlight revealed a ladder. One officer went down the ladder a step or two and located a light switch. The area below lit dankly to reveal a very large concrete bunker-type room. Pipes ran the length of the walls. Spider webs were everywhere. The officer saw what looked like piles of boxes below stacked on shelves.

The Chief addressed the group. He thanked Michelle, Maggie, Annie and Ms. Nichols for all of their input. "The book you brought along will be invaluable to this case. He smiled at Augusta. Thank you for taking time to help explain the situation we are dealing with. We would be lost without your help!" He then turned to the girls. "Girls, you all have displayed great stamina and courage investigating this situation. We thank you for your help and bravery. However, it will be best if you all leave this investigation and search effort to us, so that we don't have to worry about you ladies while we search the premises below."

Chief Graham turned to Mrs. Parks. "Since we will be sealing off the building for the investigation, would you provide the department with a set of keys?" Susan Parks left the area and returned from her office momentarily with a duplicate set of keys. She gave the keys to the Chief and told him to call her if there was anything else she could do to help the investigation. The girls and Ms. Nichols said they would be happy to help, too.

Mrs. Parks led her group back to her office. Ms. Nichols and the girls sat at the conference table with the library director. At this point, all they could do was speculate about the hidden place below the library. The excitement and comradeship, mixed with a little fear, was contagious. The group wasn't quite ready yet to leave. Mrs. Parks asked Augusta a few more questions about the zorgs, and the girls speculated about what the officers might find in the dark place beneath the library.

Meanwhile, two officers descended the ladder and searched the room beneath the trap door. The first policeman activated his radio. It crackled as the officer relayed, "Chief, there are several shelves stacked with wooden boxes. They appear to have identification labels, but the built up grime covers the lettering. They are hard to read." The second officer used his handkerchief to wipe off a label. Years of dust and cobwebs on the label began to clear. The other officer held his flashlight to read the label-"Staph Infection!" Upstairs, the Chief's expression turned from puzzlement to deep concern.

Chief Graham gave the men instructions. "Finish checking on more of the labels. Try not to disturb any of the crates. Then do a cursory search of the rest of the room and come back upstairs. Be careful, whatever you do. Wear your gloves!"

The men wiped more of the labels off and made a list. All sorts of diseases were listed on the crates. According to the labels there were stockpiles of mumps, polio, measles, and scores of other bacteria and viruses. "Bubonic Plague," the stunned officer noted, checking another box. "We have enough germs in these crates to kill millions!"

The two officers returned to the ground floor and reported to the Chief what they found in the room below. They described several hallways that appeared to lead in all directions, housing what looked like a maze of water pipes leading to the various parts of the city. They submitted the list of germs from the labels they could read. Reading over the list, the Chief realized that the case had grown beyond his jurisdiction. He needed to call in the federal authorities with an alert. This hazardous stockpile of menacing diseases secreted below his city was definitely a crisis!

The group of visitors was still in the director's office a short time later, ready to leave the building. Annie glanced through the director's office door towards the main floor of the airy building. Taking in the scores of bookshelves visible from where they sat,

Annie couldn't help pondering. "What had the zorgs been up to? How could the humans stop them?" She felt for the bulge of the big glasses in her top pocket and she was glad to have them for seeing the beasts. Suddenly, she snapped back to attention and realized that the others were preparing to leave.

"Can I call my house?" Annie asked Mrs. Parks. "I feel like checking in. I am so glad that Mrs. Cain is behind bars!" Annie dialed the number. "Hey, mom, it's me."

Annie's mom could tell something wasn't right. "Hi honey...is everything okay? I didn't expect to hear from you until tomorrow."

"I just wondered if you were OK at home," Annie answered, her voice still shaking slightly. "We found out that the creature I saw two days ago is called a zorg. Mrs. Cain, the lady from the library has something to do with it. She was arrested, and I was making sure that you are fine."

Her mom assured her. "Honey, if you are worried you can come home, but your imagination is just getting the better of you. We are fine!"

Annie suddenly felt better. "OK, Mom, I'm staying over again tonight at Michelle's. You are probably right. I love you! Oh, we're all going out to Ms. Nichols farm this afternoon. It's the farm where the creek enters the river about two miles north of town."

"Oh, I know exactly the place you are talking about. I went fishing there when I was a girl. Sure, honey, you girls have fun! I love you!" With a smile, Annie hung up the phone.

Saturday, 2:30 p.m.

His knees still a bit wobbly, the Chief of Police was unsure about what he was going to say as he dialed the Federal Bureau of Investigation's law enforcement hot-line.

"Um, my name is John Graham, Chief of Police of Battle Fork, Nebraska, and we have confirmed the presence of several alien-slash-monster creatures in our town library. We have one woman in custody who we think has a lot more information. We need your help, and please hurry, because in connection with these creatures, 'zorgs' as they are called, we have also found wooden crates containing stockpiled diseases. Each of the boxes is labeled with various pandemics such as typhoid, measles, the 1918 Spanish flu, and the bubonic plague. I planned next on calling the Centers for Disease Control and the World Health Organization to collect the poisons and dispose of the stockpile safely."

As Chief Graham hung up the phone, he realized that the CDC and WHO would not be contacted until the FBI could come and confirm that he wasn't a loon in the sticks trying to make a big scare. Hopefully, the FBI would also get a chance to see what Chief Graham was still unsure of-the presence of zorgs.

Two FBI agents arrived from the town of Ohmlink, the nearby city of 200,000, by helicopter within 40 minutes. Chief Graham explained what his men found beneath the town library. John Graham had never worked a case that required special equipment in order to locate the enemy, but he informed the government officers from the very start that a prism was required, in order to be able to see the creatures. After a twenty-minute briefing at the police station, Chief Graham, the two FBI agents, and two of Graham's officers left for the library.

The Chief brought along some of the necessary supplies for the investigation. When the patrol cars pulled to a stop in the library parking lot, Chief Graham took out the old book from the trunk that Ms. Nichols left with him earlier that day. He tucked it safely under his arm. While waiting for the FBI agents to arrive that afternoon, he had read through the book as much as he could, curious, mystified, and slightly on edge, reading about zorgs. His training many years ago as a navy SEAL hadn't been lost on him, but this time the enemy was from a different dimension!

The officer that stood guard held the door for them. Chief John Graham had his men put the supplies they brought on the floor by the secret room-flashlights, tarps, and the two hazmat suits Battle Fork ordered with Homeland Security money in 2002. The FBI agents, seated at the conference table, were each given a pair of prism eyeglasses.

Chief Graham distributed some notes about the case to the FBI agents and his own officers standing around a study table. The FBI agents skimmed the report and waited, trying to mask the look of skepticism and the wry smiles that crossed their faces.

Mrs. Parks greeted the Chief when she arrived minutes later. He asked her to be there for the upcoming meeting with the FBI, especially in regards to Mrs. Cain.

Chief Graham introduced Mrs. Parks. He took the ancient book from the table and found the page he was most interested in. He opened it to the Zorg Antidote page, and asked Mrs. Parks to carry the book around to show the agents. He explained to them they were looking at a means of controlling the invisible creatures with which the agents were about to become familiar. With no prior experience dealing with zorgs, he planned to handle this crisis with the knowledge found in the book.

The agents each took a turn looking at the old recipe from ages past when Mrs. Parks returned the book to the table beside John. The Chief addressed the group. He began by explaining the circumstances leading up to the police investigation at the library on Friday evening.

"My officers spotted lights on in the library late last night. We called Mrs. Parks to let my men into the library to investigate. Mrs. Parks, would you tell the agents what you know about all of this?"

Mrs. Parks stood in front of the group. "This all began when Annie, a twelve year old girl who comes to the library quite often, had a bike accident." She brought the story current and then referred to the ancient library book. "Several of us, including the three girls, Ms. Nichols, Chief Graham, and several officers have seen the exact creature shown in the book through a hand-held prism. We are very concerned and scared that we've come upon a dangerous situation."

The agents seemed reluctant and a bit incredulous. Chief Graham broke the silence. "Gentleman, I know this situation seems very hard to believe. Let us go now to the place we are investigating so you can examine the information yourselves."

One FBI agent and Chief Graham's deputy donned the hazmat suits. Everyone else put on a jumpsuit. The FBI intended to first verify the reported boxes of poison, and then decide their next course of action.

Before the group of investigators made moves to begin their search, Chief Graham turned to Mrs. Parks. "Mrs. Parks, your help has been invaluable. Thank you for everything you have done. We won't need your help any more today, so for safety reasons, I am going to have to ask you to leave."

Mrs. Parks nodded. "I understand, and honestly, I'm glad to be leaving. I find it difficult to think about these beasts being here all along while I'm in my office going about my daily work. It is creepy. I will be available by cell phone if you need me. You have the number." She thanked the group and left.

Chief John asked one of his officers to unseal the opening to the concealed room. The officer turned on the light and stepped back while the first FBI agent entered the hidden area behind the bookshelf. By now the officer had become used to the contraption resting on his face. He searched the room with and without the glasses. No zorgs lingered in the shadows. Then the agent opened the trap door. Other agents entered the room at this point to continue with the investigation down below. They descended the ladder in turns, and John Graham and his two deputies followed as the men gathered below.

They took an inventory of the wooden boxes stored on shelves against the basement wall. The two men wearing the hazmat suits popped the lid on the first crate they checked and found at least a hundred vials of some type of liquid in the box. A gloved hand removed a vial. The agent flashed his light on the glass vial label. It matched the label on the crate from which it had been taken, 'Botulism'. The men's faces mirrored a look of alarm.

At this point, the agents paired off. The lead FBI agent directed the groups to search down the various hallways as assigned. Chief Graham and one of his men headed down their assigned hallway. The dank corridor was dripping with cobwebs. The sticky material clung to their faces and clothes. They searched systematically. Both men had to clean and straighten their glasses as they tried to get the best view. John's partner said he was glad they had worn jumpsuits on this duty. The strong flashlight beams were almost swallowed up by the darkness. The men checked both walls and ceilings. Pipes mounted high on the basement ceiling appeared to go in all directions, dangling with cobwebs.

As his officer played the light down the hallway, Chief Graham spotted movement! Both men shone their lights in that direction-

"There!" Five or more creatures scampered around a bend and out of sight. The Chief and the officer quickly followed, shining their flashlight beams down the dark hallway. The creatures disappeared into the blackness.

"They kind of look like rats, don't they?" Chief Graham whispered, his heart pounding from the adrenaline.

"Kinda like rats," his officer replied. "But they are bigger, bulkier, and scarier-like rats on steroids." The joke was funny, but neither one of them laughed as one of the zorgs turned back and stared directly at the men. His yellow eyes glowed and the flashlights highlighted his hairy, warty, grotesque needle nose. Chief Graham and his teammate moved toward the zorg, telling the other groups of the developing situation by radio. Chief Graham described his position as best he could, trying to keep up as the zorg turned around and started to run away. No other zorgs had been spotted by the other teams. He hoped that at least one of the FBI agents would converge on their position soon. It would be best if the group could catch at least one specimen, giving credibility and resources to their dubious investigation.

Chief Graham was a tough man. Before becoming a police officer, he had been a Navy SEAL, part of a team of elite combat specialists trained in every known form of defense and warfare. However, his training had not prepared him for this. What kind of creatures were these? The Chief felt a shiver run down his spine. He suddenly wondered, "Just how do I capture one if I can catch up with it? Oh, well. No time to worry about that now!" He remembered the part about the Lord's Prayer. He began to say the prayer. He urged his fellow officer to do the same. The words were absorbed by the walls surrounding the men.

The hallway narrowed, both in width and height. They bent down and continued on, clearing cobwebs as they went. They came to a door on the left. It was stuck in place, slightly open. Chief Graham tried to push it open. He and his partner shoved against the door with their might and pushed it open. Inside on the wall to the left was a light switch. Unbelievable! The light actually worked! A thin light revealed a room with sinks and a cabinet with beakers, utensils, funnels, and other laboratory equipment, including a Bunsen burner. The room looked like it had been used recently. On sturdy shelves covering two walls were more of the wooden boxes. By now the other groups had identified Chief Graham's location and joined the Chief and his fellow officer in the strange room. They hadn't seen the fleeing zorgs. Chief Graham was disappointed-his story still needed credibility.

The men began a thorough search of the room. Hundreds of wooden packing crates lined the shelves, holding an uncounted number of vials. The Flu, Measles, Mumps, Polio, and Malaria were just a few of the labels on the outside of these boxes. Two questions were running through everyone's minds: "How had they gotten here?" and "Who bottles up germs like this?"

"We have yet to see a zorg," one FBI agent noted. "But just the presence of these vials, whether authentic or not, poses a huge threat to national security." The senior FBI agent and one of Chief Graham's officers left to contact the CDC.

Mounted on the wall beside the sink was a ladder that led to a platform above that served as a walk way. The walkway gave access to the dozens of pipes that converged in this room into a hub-like structure. A massive diagram of the pipes hung above the hub. Each pipe had been numbered, and was identified by colored paint or tape, as well as on its respective route through the maze on the map. In the center of the hub of pipes was a device that you could open to add material to the water in the pipes. According to the diagram, these pipes had been discreetly tunneled and fused to different water supply pipes as water was distributed throughout the city. Chief Graham thought it odd that the public works department had yet to uncover any of this sabotage when fixing the water main breaks that often occurred during the harsh winters, but then concluded that everything about these zorgs, for some reason, is partially hidden. Chief Graham spotted a small handle, and pushed it down. The device opened, waiting for something to be added to the water flowing inside.

Boxes and boxes of the vials were stacked near the device. This adapter was waiting in this hidden section of the city's underbelly for the sole purpose of poisoning people! This evil place made the Chief feel ill. He felt nauseous and claustrophobic. Where did these vials come from? How did someone (or something) obtain these contaminations and multiply them into such an astonishing number? This operation must rival the CDC's operations in saving virus samples to fight possible future pandemics-but in this case, the zorgs want to create one? And why, so far had this small town escaped certain doom? Were the zorgs planning a "trial run" anytime soon? Another shudder ran along the Chief's spine.

The group said very little, but the look on their faces said it all. They decided to return to the library and make a report to headquarters. When the men got back upstairs, a higher ranking FBI officer was already there. A large group of FBI, CDC, and Hazmat removal teams were scheduled to arrive as soon as possible. The FBI agents insisted on staying in the building until help arrived.

Chief Graham returned to the police station. His understanding of reality had changed in less than twenty four hours. He reached for his list of city and state numbers. Locating the person he needed to call, he dialed the number. Chief Graham realized that this investigation would be much larger than his small town. The Chief knew he might be able to help the investigation best by securing the "old town" information, in order to speed up this strange investigation.

"Hello?-Brian! John Graham here. I know it's the weekend, but I need you to check all of the blueprints on file for structural renovations to the buildings in this town. What I'm looking for is mainly associated with plumbing changes to the downtown area. Please make a record of the building code changes, including sewer and water mains, since this town was first built over a hundred years ago. I know it's a big order, but we have a situation. Get your maps and meet me at the police headquarters as soon as possible! Sorry to interrupt your day off!" John hung up the phone. That at least was a beginning, one thing that might help jump-start this investigation. Brian Raymond, the City Clerk, would locate every blueprint on file in the County Records Office dealing with the underground structures.

Saturday, 3:35 p.m.

The summer sky held a few puffy white clouds. A slight breeze was rustling the leaves of the trees along the street where Michelle and Ms. Nichols lived. Annie felt a sense of adventure as they gathered up the bag of equipment for their trip to the farm to collect the materials needed for the zorg antidote. The girls followed Ms. Nichols out to her garage.

She backed the car out of its resting place and the girls piled in. They headed north out of town. Trees were plentiful along the skyline to the east where the river wound. The corn they passed along the highway was almost mature. The wind waved the tassels gracefully. In a couple of months the combines would clear these corn fields, and once again the view would be clear for miles. In the distance the sun reflected on the hillsides. Cattle grazed lazily in their pastures. Annie and her friends had come past this place hundreds of times, but for the first time they noticed the slight road to the right side of the highway.

Ms. Nichols turned down the dirt lane and headed east. The road wound to the north of the cornfield, along a slough, and passed a couple of ponds on its way to the western border of the river. The lane dropped down an embankment and up to the other side. She glided the car to a stop in the grassy clearing. The area was surrounded by huge cottonwood trees, a host of other kinds of trees and ground cover. Augusta put the car in park and turned off the engine.

Annie carried a plastic gallon jug and Maggie and Michelle each had two of the quart jars for the water. Ms. Nichols picked up the burlap sack that held the extra prisms she'd brought along for making the antidote, a container of salt, a teaspoon to measure the salt and moss, and paring knives. Ms. Nichols told the girls that when she was a child, her parents and she would come here for picnics and bring sleeping bags and spend the night. Annie reminded the group about their prism glasses. They put them on and looked around at the surrounding area.

The newcomers walked to a clearing that looked out on the river. The wind whispered through the tree branches. The birds sang. The water gurgled. They reached the picnic table where Ms. Nichols set the contents of the burlap bag. Nearby was a small one-room cabin nestled in the trees overlooking the water.

Ms. Nichols gave the girls a short tour of the riverbank. She pointed out where the creek used to flow, but told them that a few years before, the river had changed naturally. The creek now channeled into the river further to the south. She'd gone swimming in a big pond that used to be there when she was growing up. The girls took off their shoes and socks and walked out onto the sandy river bottom. The water was clear and cool. It felt good this hot summer afternoon. After a few minutes the girls climbed up the bank and returned to the picnic table. They picked up the quart jars and ran back out to the sandbar and filled the jars with the swirling water.

They set the full containers down in front of where Augusta waited, relaxing in the pleasant surroundings. A host of native birds flitted about, unaccustomed to the commotion of company in the normally vacant woods. The girls sat at the table and brushed the sand off of their dry feet. They put on their socks and shoes while Ms. Nichols waited for them.

The first thing Augusta did was give the girls mosquito spray and sun block from the cabin. When the girls were done applying all their outdoor protection, Ms. Nichols told them to explore the cabin. They scanned the twelve-by-eighteen foot shed. There was a big wood stove in the center of a kitchen area. In the middle of the big room were a small table and several chairs. At the back of the cabin was a sleeping area. The windows were covered with curtains. Annie pulled back a panel covering the glass. The three looked out at the beautiful scene, where the sprawling Moosehorn River rolled past the cabin, then curled around in the distance, and continued in an south-eastern direction around the big bend. The Battle Fork Creek joined the body of water to the south of the bend.

Annie put on her prism glasses, sort of jokingly, as if the place was hiding a zorg. The others did that too. Laughing, the group exited the building and returned to the picnic table where Augusta had separated the supplies for each girl.

Ms. Nichols gave each girl a plastic container and a paring knife. These were their tools for gathering moss. They followed her down a slight trail into the woods. She found a suitable place and set her equipment down on a big fallen tree trunk. Finding a good place to sit down, Augusta took her paring knife and, with the other hand held her container below a spot on the wood.

"Girls, this is what we need to do." She began to flick the greenish-brown moss off of the old bark. She worked quickly and diligently for a couple of minutes, demonstrating how to scrape flakes of moss off of the wood. "With all of us working, it shouldn't take very long to find enough to make a big batch of the recipe that we need. Let's spread out. Be sure to avoid any plants with leaves of three, like poison ivy or poison oak. Remember, leaves of three, leave them be."

The three girls took their equipment and fanned out. Annie passed a thick stand of trees to a place where she could sit down while she worked. She started scraping the moss, listening to the soothing sound of the river in the distance. Lost in her thoughts, she was surprised by a sound. Annie adjusted the glasses. She looked through the prism glasses, and was astonished to see a figure that could only be described as an elf standing nearby. He was visible through the prism! She looked above the glasses, and was surprised that she could still see the elf without the prism!

"Hello, little lady!" he grinned. "I am pleased to make your acquaintance. My name is Magnus. I'm sorry to have startled you! Don't be afraid. I couldn't help but notice that you are wearing a prism on those eyeglass frames. You look a bit strange, and I must say, funny." The elf was still smiling. "What exactly are you doing? Are you scraping moss from that tree bark?"

Annie sat for a moment, stunned. "I am here with some friends and the lady that brought us out here. Her family owns this farm. Her name is Augusta Nichols. She is somewhere nearby, also gathering moss. It would be good to let her know that you are here."

"Splendid!" replied Magnus.

A part of Annie was not surprised as she picked up her partially filled container and the paring knife. The two unlikely companions backtracked to where Annie last saw Ms. Nichols. Augusta was still there, with moss almost to the top of her container. She heard the rustle of leaves and looked up. A smile spread across her face when she saw them.

"Annie, you have an elf with you!" she exclaimed. Annie held her prism glasses and introduced Magnus to her mentor.

The elf was dressed in leather boots that came up to his knees, where they folded over and formed the shape of an inverted "V." He wore a leather vest and dark green trousers, with a bright red silk shirt tucked in at the waist. He had a goatee and mustache, and light brown hair. His face was jovial, putting Annie at ease. Annie had never seen a more fascinating figure. He wore an old fashioned Robin Hood cap with an eagle feather off to the side of its band. There was a knife at his belt. He had the strap of his backpack over his shoulder.

Augusta stood up and hugged the little elf. Magnus blushed. "I'm sorry if I have embarrassed you. I can't help it! You are so cute!" Augusta exclaimed. The other girls heard the talking and came running. Magnus shook the excited girls' hands. He told them he had been in this very neighborhood when Augusta was a girl and knew of her father.

"Augusta, I couldn't help but notice your friend here, Annie, collecting moss. Then I saw you gathering moss. What is going on?" he asked.

Augusta replied, "Magnus, I believe you know what a zorg is."

"Oh, goodness! Do I ever! Have you been so unfortunate as to find one of these beasts?"

Augusta nodded. "Annie had a bike accident Wednesday morning. Inadvertently she saw a zorg. I'd just met her friend, Maggie, the day before. When Annie asked Maggie what to do, Maggie told her to talk to me. It just so happened that my father had given me all of his old books. I went through them long ago, but after my father died, I left them in storage. It was so strange! I retrieved the books from the farm only last week, and had just begun to sort through them at my home in town. When Annie told me what happened to her, and showed me a drawing she'd made of this creature, I found her the book that mentioned the zorgs. As you must know, usually people aren't able to see zorgs without a prism, but Annie's tears, along with the reflection in a store-front window made it possible for her to see one with her own eyes!"

"How coincidental that you met Annie after reviewing the box of books from your father." Magnus replied. "God works in mysterious ways!" The elf smiled at his new friends. "I came to this place today specifically to check on the area. We have a portal nearby that gives access to this dimension from our realm. Our world is parallel to this one. Unfortunately, we share it with the zorgs. The zorgs on our side have been acting a bit peculiar for a few days now, so we have been monitoring the earth for any alarming activity, as well. We've doubled the number of elves on the patrol schedules for greater security and protection in our realm.

I must admit, this is a pleasant surprise. Life for us elves has been very intense lately. I was totally unprepared to find you people gathering moss for the antidote used against the zorgs. I knew exactly what you were making and knew that you must be friendly. I am so glad to see you girls working on the antidote. We cannot make the solution from ingredients from our world. The water and salt and moss must come from this world."

Annie could tell that Magnus thoroughly enjoyed his captive audience. "Let me give you a little history lesson, ladies. The zorgs have battled the elves since the beginning of the world. According to elven lore, however, one day the battle will change drastically. Man and elf will fight together against the zorgs in our dimension. Up until that predetermined time, elves are unable to communicate with man, and man cannot see elves, much less enter the portal between our two words. So, in case you haven't figured it out yet, I have a huge reason to smile. The elves are ready, anxious, and eager to meet their human comrades. And now I can say I have met four of them!

The elven prophecy claimed that once the 'Great Breach' occurred, not only would humans be able to see the elves clearly, but humans would also be able to enter our realm and participate in the battle of good against evil in zorg territory. Elves have hoped on this day for generations! After creating us, God assigned us to patrol the nether world; to mitigate the power and number of zorgs. It has always been an honor for every elf from the beginning of creation to serve God's Will." However, in recent times the zorg population has grown stronger than our ability to keep it in check.

God's timing is wonderful! I would have never believed it one week ago, or even two days ago, that I would be talking today to humans! I feel so blessed that I am here talking to you!"

Magnus continued, "Tell me everything so far that has happened! I want to be able to understand the events that brought you here today."

Annie began the story by telling Magnus what happened to her three days prior when the old librarian tried to frighten Maggie and her. Then Annie and Maggie explained what happened the day they went back with Annie to get her library card. They described Mrs. Cain's mean-spirited meltdown, the zorg tattoo on her hand and the black shadow surrounding her when Annie saw her through the prism, and the kindness and open-mindedness of Mrs. Parks. But things become even more interesting, Annie noted, when Mrs. Parks called the girls the very next morning regarding a possible zorg infestation of the library.

Magnus interjected, "How strange it is that her name is Cain! There has been an old saying among elves since the earliest days of the Earth, back when Adam and Eve had all that trouble with their two sons. It goes, 'The last thing you need if you're Able is a Cain!'" He grinned.

"One of your predecessors had a sense of humor! You are such fun!" Augusta replied with a smile.

Annie continued with her story. "That same afternoon we accidentally found Mrs. Cain's house and witnessed her hiding some books and prisms. Also, the book she had taken away from us at the library was there. When we took it to Ms. Nichols and had time to explore the book's pages, we found the section related to the subject of zorgs and the recipe for the zorg antidote. The police now have the old book and a bunch of Holy Bibles that Mrs. Cain hid under her porch. They are using the information found in the old book during the investigation. Right after we watched her hide the things in her yard, we saw a zorg go to the same spot where she hid them under the porch."

Annie continued. "The police saw lights on and investigated a possible break-in at the library late last night. Mrs. Parks, the director, was called downtown to open the building for the police. She already knew, from us talking with her yesterday, that a prism reveals the zorg's presence. So when the police called the Director last night when they saw the unusual lights on, she had the officers look through the prism that she kept locked in her desk. It freaked the cops out to see ugly creatures scampering around the hidden room where they also found Mrs. Cain."

"That was how the police got involved." Ms. Nichols added. "Now more agencies have been called in. It seems the zorgs have access to the city water supply and the means to contaminate it with a stockpile of bacteria and viruses. We offered to help the chief by collecting ingredients for the zorg antidote. Now the girls and I are gathering this moss for the recipe described in the book."

Magnus listened to the story with his full attention. After Augusta finished speaking, Magnus thanked them all for telling him what was happening in the human dimension. "The situation in our neighborhood led us to wonder if this 'Great Breach' had finally occurred," Magnus noted. "I came through the portal today to record zorg activity. The zorgs have been unusually busy on our side the last twenty-four hours. We are seeing things that don't make any sense. Zorgs, creatures of darkness, are congregating freely during daylight hours. Zorgs have been migrating back to the Czorg palace from all regions of the earth. They have doubled the number of guards around their castle. They have been carrying small crates to and from their various portals-we can only assume they are making deliveries of vile materials to their network across the earth. And, oddly enough, we have discovered cases of frenzied zorgs burning weaker zorgs as sacrifices. As these carcasses burn, greenish-brown smoke fills the air and a most putrid smell lingers for hours after the fire is gone. As some of you may already know, zorgs don't walk around smelling like a flower, but I must say, any stench they emit is a cakewalk compared to the smell of their burning flesh. Just thinking about the smell makes me want to vomit."

Magnus continued. "The zorgs are obviously being summoned by the Czorg from the far reaches of our region. Normally zorgs are nocturnal creatures. They hide like rats. Now they are acting like rabid animals, foaming at the mouth, almost crazed.

The zorgs have always operated at will among humans, as invisible creatures. However, though this may seem like a dark and scary time, we have reason to hope. Now that several police officers have seen the zorgs and the diseases they have stockpiled, the 'Great Breach' has occurred. It is sure to be a fight for zorg survival, since the humans are aware of their existence and will try to destroy them.

Centuries ago, when Galileo discovered a zorg in his lab, fear gripped the zorg community. The zorgs believed then that the "Great Breach" had occurred. The Czorg was petrified. He was sure his demise had arrived, and spent all of his efforts fortifying his palace and hiding. It was strange when Galileo's discovery never made the news! We prayed for his strength to persevere through the attacks in his career, and without his knowledge, we pampered his horses and made sure his ink never ran out while he wrote his thesis. We made sure that each copy of his thesis made it to its destination in the church and scientific communities. Yet, nothing happened. The Czorg soon realized he had nothing to fear. He used the skepticism to his advantage and sent zorgs to claim the souls of Galileo's critics."

Magnus looked sternly at the girls. "Don't ever let any arrogance affect your intellect. Always be open-minded and please, please, do the research to understand the 'why' of what you believe. Don't believe something just because someone tells you to, because your parents are that way, or because on the surface it seems reasonable. Such ignorant tactics make you vulnerable to the zorgs and ultimately to Satan. Even in loving the Lord your God as Creator, be vigilant. Read God's Word. Seek the Truth through prayer and meditation. Remember, the state of your soul should be the most important consideration you ever undertake."

Magnus' furrowed brows now became light-hearted. "I apologize for the tangent. Just think of me as a cute little elf that is looking out for you. Now, where was I? We were talking about the Czorg. Here's some trivia for ya'. You have heard the stories from your book that Galileo had named the intruder in his laboratory a 'zorg'. The leader of the zorgs was so arrogant that he enjoyed now having a human name. He decided that he could parrot the title of the earthly Russian leader, called a 'Czar' with 'zorg' to come up with his own very special title-the 'Czorg.' We were very sad to see the 'Czorg' come out of hiding acting more powerful only a short time later. He sent zorgs out with trumpets throughout our land, announcing his new title. The sound of his name makes elves sick."

"The zorgs realize what a huge liability Mrs. Cain is. Her carelessness and defensiveness with Annie led to the zorg's discovery as a human threat. Honestly, if she would have left you girls alone with that book in the library, Annie's story may have never gained credibility. No offense, Annie, it is just hard to take a twelve-year old's eyewitness account about an invisible creature too seriously. Now that Mrs. Cain is in prison, I am sure the zorgs are coming up with every possible strategy to rid themselves of her."

Magnus continued. "Would you be interested in accompanying me to my world? Never before has any human set foot there, but now that the 'Great Breach' has occurred, humans can enter there. I would like you to visit our world and tell my fellow elves exactly what, so far, has transpired."

The girls chimed in. "Yes!"

Augusta was a bit more reserved. "Will it take long?" she asked.

Magnus replied, "Our castle is close to this portal. It shouldn't take very long. I will see to it that you are safe. They have not yet dared to attack our castle. I suspect today would be a safe time for you to visit since they are in chaos now and have Mrs. Cain to deal with."

"I am a little concerned," Ms. Nichols replied. "I am responsible for these girls' safety."

"Let me tell you," Magnus said, "it seems that the zorgs already know who you are. It is possible that a few of them might even be watching us right now, though well-hidden. They may even be orchestrating a booby trap as you make your way back to your car. What I am saying is that, right now, you are probably as safe with me in our world as you are here, collecting moss. We can mix up the ingredients for the solution you are preparing and let it sit in the sun while we are gone. We should be back about the same time the antidote is ready."

Ms. Nichols agreed, still looking apprehensive.

"Good! Let's collect the moss from everyone's container." said Magnus. The girls ran and grabbed their containers. They met at the picnic table. "Let's see how much we've got." Between them they had almost a full gallon container of the green flakes.

"That should be enough to make several quarts of the solution. Do you think this is enough for now?" Augusta asked Magnus.

"Oh, that should do nicely for a good while. Only a small amount of the antidote is required. A spray of the water solution into the air near any zorg will diminish his capabilities immediately. It is uncanny how strongly the zorgs respond to this formula," Magnus replied.

"I think it has to do with the fact that the moss is basically a physical shadow. It grows in the shade and somehow, using the moss with saltwater affects the zorgs. Salt is the universal antiseptic, and it cleans out all forms of disease. A zorg's system cannot tolerate it. The prism, with its three sides, represents the Holy Trinity: the Father, the Son, and the Holy Spirit. Water, the ingredient that was turned into wine by Our Lord during his very first public miracle all those years ago, is a constant reminder to the zorgs and the devil that their fate is sealed. They know that they are doomed. What a symbolic antidote we have then, hey? Don't forget the power punch of the Lord's Prayer as a weapon, too, right?" grinned the mischievous elf. "We sing that prayer on our daily rounds and it seems to drive the zorgs crazy. They run for the deep brush, the hills, wherever, as deep as the darkness will hide them. They despise those words!" he shook his head. "They hate the very name of Jesus!"

Magnus looked up at the sky. The sun shone brightly. The clouds were gone. It was perfect weather for making the antidote. Ms. Nichols added the measured amount of moss and salt to the water in each of the four jars the girls had filled from the river earlier. She carefully placed a prism into each jar, and finally put a lid on all four jars before giving each one a spin. She then arranged them in the center of the picnic table.

Magnus said, "Why don't we move this table over so that it stays out of the shade while we are gone?" They moved it further over to the clearing. Maggie and Annie gathered up the remaining supplies and put them into the gunnysack. They carried the bag back to Ms. Nichols' car.

Ms. Nichols called out to the two girls, "Would you mind bringing the apples and the water jug along when you come back? They're on the floor of the backseat. Thanks!" Annie emptied the sack onto the front seat and put the water jug and the paper bag full of apples into the empty gunny sack. The two girls practically ran back to the picnic table. Everyone was excited and ready to see the elves' castle.

Magnus said, "We'll just leave the jars on the table for a while. By the time we get back the antidote will be ready. Let's hope the zorgs leave it alone." The troop headed out like a gaggle of girl scouts. They headed north on a thin trail through the tall growth in the woods. The smell of the greenery and trees left a fresh aroma. The party traveled north for a short while. Soon Magnus put his arm out to stop the procession.

"Wait. Here is the place!"

Soon Magnus put his arm out to stop the steady progression. He said, "Wait. Here is the place!"

He stepped behind a magnificent cottonwood tree near a slight cliff and vanished! The girls walked around the entire tree where he disappeared. No Magnus anywhere!

"He's gone!" Annie exclaimed. Ms. Nichols smiled to herself, thinking this was some kind of elven prank.

"Girls, you heard everything Magnus said today. Why would he just disappear? He is our friend. We'll wait. I'm sure he will be back!"

Just then Magnus spoke to them. "I'm right here. I wanted to let my sentry know that I was bringing company and that I planned to give you a tour of our side of the world. He sent a dispatch pigeon to inform the castle of our impending visit. They will be waiting. Follow me!"

Magnus took Ms. Nichols' hand and suddenly disappeared as he leaned into the center of the huge tree trunk. Augusta still held his hand, but he was gone! Augusta leaned into the same place where Magnus had been. Suddenly she was somewhere else, still holding hands.

The three girls watched Augusta as she merged into the center of the tree and disappeared. The onlookers did the same thing and one by one, they passed through the portal.

A uniformed elf stood at attention at the gateway, wide eyed. Magnus introduced the humans to Gary. The elf sentry gave them a salute and a shy smile. The girls giggled at his sweet sight. They were standing in a little portal office carved out of rocks. Magnus showed the newcomers around the guard post.

"This is our little kitchen area. Through that doorway is the barracks. Sometimes we are on duty for long stretches at a time. The guards rotate shifts. Andy, one of our other sentry guards, was sent on reconnaissance rounds early this morning."

These are the means by which we communicate with the castle and others in our realm." Magnus pointed out flags stored in a barrel in the corner. "Colored flags have meanings. Red means zorgs have been spotted and things are amiss. Yellow means there is a poison scare, or a zorg is suspected of bringing in poisons from your world. Other colors have various meanings. Our castle is within sight of all the portals. We can also signal the castle from here by candle lanterns at night, or use mirrors during the day. The big drum stored in the corner we use any time, to contact the entire surrounding area of some major threat, like a fire. Oh, and also, the animals communicate thoughts to us through telepathy."

Magnus walked the newcomers to the aviary built against a wall by the desk and message supplies. It had a glass front and a walk-in doorway. The perches were made of natural branches and along one side were food and water dishes. Many pigeons cooed at them, and some sat beside their mates, carefully watching the group. One or two took short trips across the cage to change positions.

"Our dispatch pigeons travel back and forth with specific details of our operations. They are also used to transport smaller items to and from the castle." Leather pouches with small straps were piled in a basket. There was a stack of paper, an ink bottle, and a quill pen on the small desk.

Annie, feeling nauseous and claustrophobic, stepped outside of the cramped elven post. She looked at a trail that had been worn into the landscape by frequent use. In her mind's eye she could imagine the elves making the rounds. She imagined a scene of these elves frequenting the woods, coming and going to Ms. Nichols' family farm all the while. She smiled, thinking that her nearby town two miles south had no clue that any of this was happening.

She looked around. The place was surrounded by big boulders and a crop of rocks that served as a giant wall.

"The terrain in this realm is nothing like the world we just left! Weird!" Annie thought. She stepped back into to the doorway. "Magnus, can you tell me why the landscape is so different on this side from our world?"

Magnus grinned. "The two worlds don't correspond with the same landscape. Humans have actually built structures on some of the portals to your world, but we are still able to pass through, like little mice." He grinned at the girls.

Magnus continued to speak. "In this world you don't need those glasses to see the zorgs. Here zorgs are in plain sight." The girls took off the contraptions. Augusta reached into the burlap sack as she asked if anyone wanted a drink of water. Everybody took a drink before she put the water jug back into the gunnysack. She took the bag of apples out and gave one to everyone, including little Gary. There were just enough for everyone. Augusta took off her glasses and put them into the paper bag. She held it open for Maggie, Annie and Michelle, and they each set their glasses into the bag. Augusta rolled the bag closed and put it back into the burlap sack, on top of the partially full water jug.

They took bites from their apples as Magnus continued, "This world is a lot different than yours." He took another bite of his red apple and chewed it for a minute before he continued. "One difference is that you can't run engines or man-made electronic devices on this side. We have no phones or electricity here." Magnus finished the apple and stood up. "Thank you, Augusta. That hit the spot!" he said. They all agreed. Leading them outside, he pointed across the valley and identified a place on the far hillside where a castle shone in the sun. "That is where we are headed. That is the elven castle."

They could see the trail that wound down through the valley below and up the other side to the castle gates.

"It is less than two miles away. Not far at all! If everyone is ready, let's go!" he said, anxious to get his visitors to meet the elders at the governing hall. The elder elves and the administrators were gathering information and would be anticipating their arrival. After all, this was a monumental event. The first humans ever to enter their realm were expected at the castle! Magnus had butterflies in his stomach from the excitement!

Everyone said goodbye to Gary. Trailing behind Magnus, the others filed out of the cramped surroundings. They were out in the sunshine again. Magnus guided Augusta and the others followed behind, as he found his way along the path towards the valley below. They traveled along a small canyon. It wasn't very long before this trail made a gradual decent to the lowland. They crossed over a stream on a tiny bridge. Magnus kept his voice to a whisper when they reached the tree line.

A slight breeze rustled through the trees. A foul odor drifted to the travelers noses. "Ugh," Michelle coughed. It made them all feel queasy. Annie dry heaved. The stench was terrible. It took a few moments for her to compose herself. Annie looked up. Michelle, Maggie, and Ms. Nichols all had their noses under their shirts. Annie did the same.

Magnus declared, "That smell, my friends, is the odor of burning zorg. There must be a ritual going on nearby up-wind. "It's hard to say what is going on today. Normally the zorgs conduct their business under cover of darkness. These woods are always a bit dangerous since they provide cover for lurking intruders. A careful watch will be required now that we have reached the trees!"

"We elves have discovered the shield prayer provides us, especially when we enter dangerous, dark, or unfamiliar territory. Elves have learned to repeat the Lord's Prayer as a means of defense. Prayers are like the energy that is stored in a battery. When our prayers wind their way to the heavens, they recharge the spiritual battery. This energy drives the spiritual defense mechanism that curtails evil. This energy increases the angels' strength in their battles with evil. It helps humans as well as the elves to shield and overcome the dangers of darkness. The entire universe is involved in the drama that has been unfolding on the planet Earth for all time. This spiritual battery is the power source available to angels and all of the spiritual forces sent to rescue the earth. When the battery is low, the chaos and problems on this planet multiply, like the zorgs.

"Strong prayer shakes the patterns of evil loose and allows positive situations to replace the weed of evil that was in its place. The events here in our world are reflected in your world. When the zorg population increases, crime soars in your world. A delicate balance exists that must be met in order to maintain enough spiritual energy to fuel the battle against the evil that tries to disrupt mankind through sin.

"It all began and ended one day in heaven. I'm speaking of the day that God, after so loving and admiring one of his favorite angels, Lucifer, knew that He had created a monster. God's favor and attention filled the handsome angel with pride. Lucifer was beautiful. He was musical. He was intelligent. Instead of recognizing his talents as gifts and thanking God for them, Lucifer became arrogant and started to resent God's omnipotent role. His pride refused to worship God one terrible day, and God's punishment as he threw Lucifer from heaven has permeated the very fabric of time.

"God knew what He was saying when He admonished people to discipline their children. It is a sad development when one's own child defies you. On that fateful day, the arrogant and selfish Angel Lucifer and a third of the heavens fell from God's grace. Lucifer actually committed the very first sin. Because of this, the heavens erupted. The defiant angels that sided with Lucifer were ejected, to dwell in the far darkness of the universe to perpetrate their deeds until the final battle: the dominion of good over evil. Now that this 'Great Breach' has occurred, we are all one step closer to the culmination of God's plan."

The troop made their way through the wooded hillside, winding on a trail that Magnus knew well. They conversed in hushed tones, Magnus trying to educate the newcomers of the history and the ways of his world.

"We can be notified of events by the birds and animals, as we pick up on their perceptions. The birds and animals even come up with ideas on their own to thwart the zorgs. For instance, the birds will swoop down and pull the hair out of the zorg's head when they catch one traveling out in the open. Cats can attack a zorg, and nine times out of ten, are able to slash the zorg's throat with their superior hunting skills within seconds. Dogs allow us to ride on their backs to chase and catch the zorgs, and they also patrol our forests. See those birds way up there?" Magnus pointed upward. There were several eagles circling high above the mountains.

"Yes!" the girls said together.

Magnus continued, "Earlier today they spotted a nest of zorgs and sent images of a trail heavily populated by zorgs, traveling towards the Czorg Palace, yonder maybe ten miles.

A huge battle is brewing. We constantly patrol our portals since we suspect that the zorgs might be trying to bring in tainted items. In desperation, they use the vile germs from your world as a tool. They scramble to corrupt as many humans as possible, before the final battle."

Ahead the sunshine penetrated the thinning branches. Before long they could see the castle above them through the branches. It was a golden color with a drawbridge, almost glowing from the sunshine. Much of the structure was overgrown with ivy. A stone path led up to the entrance of the castle gates. There were four towers surrounded by a wall. Annie looked carefully about herself as they made their way. She thought she saw two zorgs just past the tree line, studying their every move. She felt like she was living in a fiction novel. And despite all of Magnus' reassurance, she still prayed that there would be a happy ending.

Saturday, 3:59 p.m.

Chief John Graham had not been able to slow down since last night's discovery. His men discovered more of the infectious vials at Buanna Cain's house earlier in the day.

Something huge was underfoot, and it seemed that the hub of activity, at least with what they knew of now, was right here. This thing had to be bigger than just this city, though, and only through an organized approach could the country and world prevent the zorgs' plans from coming to fruition.

Training had prepared him for the larger scope of events, and he did not doubt for a minute that these creatures were everywhere on earth. With a little luck he hoped that mankind could stop the advance of the invisible enemy, now that they had been alerted. He thanked God that Annie had come across the first known zorg, because that incident had made the terrible discovery possible. He was grateful for Ms. Nichols' input. He wondered what path they would have taken had she not been there to help educate them all about the zorgs.

It had been a long time since he'd met anyone as interesting as Ms. Augusta Nichols. If he could get this problem resolved before they were all destroyed, his first plan was to ask her for a date. The words even sounded strange to him. He had put things of the heart out of his mind almost twenty years ago when the love of his life was killed only weeks before they were to be married. No woman had interested him since then. His career in the service, and then in the police force, had taken up all of his time for the past two decades. It was hard for him to believe that Augusta had lived in this town all that time and he never knew that she existed.

Augusta had told him that she planned to take the girls out to her farm to look for moss for the antidote against the zorgs. He'd driven past that farm for years. He'd never met her before, though. His mind was distracted as he wondered what the girls were doing right then. He hoped that they were safe. Augusta had given him directions to where she planned to be. If they didn't make it back home safely, he could go look for them. He would try calling them at Augusta's home later.

Chief Graham hadn't eaten and decided to take a short break for a bite to eat. He walked to the small refrigerator next to the water fountain in the police department kitchen and removed the sack lunch he'd brought that morning. He had made a tuna sandwich and he brought two hardboiled eggs and some carrots. He peeled the eggs by the sink and rinsed off the little particles of shells left on the slippery white orbs. He stopped at the coffeepot and refilled the mug he was holding in his left hand. Grabbing the saltshaker, he returned to his desk, looking over the notes he'd scribbled earlier. He ate the first hardboiled egg. He was starved and he realized that it had been several hours since he'd eaten that bowl of cereal and grapefruit at seven o'clock this morning.

John opened his top desk drawer, took out a notebook and began to compile a list of everything that he knew about the case, making a separate page for what he knew about the zorgs and another page for Mrs. Cain. He ate his sandwich as he wrote, and then finished off the last hardboiled egg and a carrot. He concentrated on the pages as his pencil flew over the paper.

A sergeant knocked on John's office door, interrupting his thoughts. The young police officer announced to the Chief that some of the FBI agents had returned from the library. He asked his officer to lead the group to the conference room. There the FBI and Center for Disease Control agents converged at the large table and started sharing information.

Initial introductions were made and the senior agent for the FBI team, Pete Jacobs, began the meeting. "The danger we have uncovered is even more deadly than governmental officials first feared," the FBI team leader began. "We have shipped samples of the vials to a nearby lab for testing, to be certain that the labels on the vials are accurate. We are in the middle of an arduous process to recover all of these vials. Issue a notice to the citizens immediately, to drink and cook with only bottled water. I would recommend the temporary evacuation of this city on Monday morning, in effect until all of the vials have been removed and the water supply has been flushed and tested.

"The evidence from the search of the library will be transported by truck to the Center for Disease Control headquarters, escorted by a military patrol. We have sent bulletins to every FBI agent in the country. More alerts are being wired around the world. We have issued a bulletin to all federal and state government offices as well. The homeland security alert will be raised within the day to its highest level, red, once we have useful information to provide the public. Internally, we have implemented a routine check of all personnel for signs of the telltale zorg tattoo. We realize the possibility of zorg helpers among us. The President has been on the phone with world leaders in order to coordinate a response to this threat."

Pete spoke to his assistant, Josh, seated near Chief Graham. "Show the Chief the photo we got by fax just a while ago." The agent passed him a photograph of the zorg tattoo on Buanna Cain's hand. "Our lab was able to attach a prism to the camera to get this picture."

"The FBI continues looking into the phone records of Buanna Cain, which are strangely long and extensive, given that she has no immediate family as stated on her employment forms. We are looking for the connection between her and these individuals. So far,

Mrs. Cain has refused to answer any questions. We hope she will cooperate with us to avert any further problems. The army has dispatched troops to gather moss immediately. A task force is locating prisms from stores and factories."

John had brought the notes he'd compiled over his late lunch. He sketched a drawing of the prism glasses. After checking over the lists he'd compiled and finishing his drawing, he handed the pages over to his assistant and asked him to make copies for the agents. A copy was also sent by fax to FBI headquarters. FBI agent Josh would serve as liaison between the FBI and the Pentagon for military action.

When the meeting ended, John gave the agents a tour of the police department, including the next room with the recliner and couch, for their use if they needed a break. Walking them past the bathroom, he led them to the kitchen. He told them they were welcome to help themselves to the fruit, sandwiches and the beverages in the refrigerator, and pointed out the restaurant guide posted on the bulletin board.

"Stay away from the water out of the faucets." John forced a smile. "We have plenty of bottled water for you in the fridge."

John made sure that his guests were comfortable, and then called his dispatcher and told him to beef up the patrol for the homes of those involved in the altercation with the librarian. "Make sure that the officers know how to use the prism glasses!" John returned to his office and studied the blueprints on his desk.

Brian, the City Clerk, had delivered the blueprints of the city's downtown buildings. Some of them dated back to the eighteen hundreds. There seemed to be a discrepancy in the records delineating structural changes to some of the buildings from around the early 1900's. That was when the city built the sewer system. The clerk noticed that the blueprints for that time period had disappeared, including those of the police department and the hospital. John and two FBI agents conducted an emergency meeting with the mayor and city council. He briefed them on the zorg threat. While in the meeting, John received an important phone call. Initial water quality testing at the sanitation plant showed no evidence of sabotage. The group breathed a collective sigh of relief. The FBI agents urged the city leaders to remain calm and to not evacuate. Any panic or hysteria stemming from this crises would only divert valuable resources from fighting the zorgs.

The FBI now had several men guarding the water and power companies, all wearing zorg glasses, and was strategically positioned to watch for other targets that may be sabotaged. John had been correct in discerning that there might be a route to the hospital from the maze of hallways where he had discovered the underground lab. Zorgs had been collecting tissue samples for years. The FBI had found the well-worn route just hours before.

The phone rang. Chief Graham answered, and then put the conversation on speaker phone. The agent on the phone identified himself as Steven Dean from Washington, D.C. "I just left the cell where Buanna Cain is being questioned. Up until twenty minutes ago, our questioning was very unfruitful. The woman clammed up completely. However, by checking Buanna Cain's phone records, one of the numbers we traced led to Mrs. Huber. She has been questioned. She is the wife of the man that Buanna often called. She said she knew Buanna Cain and she thought her horrible. She overheard many of her husband's conversations with Mrs. Cain and she begged her husband to stop his association with her. He was a plumber by trade. He worked on the city pipes often, and for some reason, Buanna Cain had something over him. Huber was afraid to tell her 'No'. He disappeared several days ago, and she hasn't heard from him. That isn't too unusual, though, because he often gets held over in remote places, working on the pipe systems to reservoirs. Sometimes he doesn't get service on his cell phone until he gets near a populated town somewhere. He didn't tell her he expected to be gone for this long. But now, since we showed up, she became afraid. She said, 'He told me only a couple of weeks ago that if something ever happened to him, to give this letter to the police.'"

Agent Steven Dean's voice started reading the letter. "'To Whom This May Concern: I, Kyle Jace Huber, must make a confession. Mrs. Cain gave me a thousand dollars to install unauthorized plumbing beneath the library. I was deep in debt, paying family bills, sending my son to college, and the money seemed like a godsend. After I installed the equipment, Mrs. Cain wouldn't leave me alone. There are strange things going on with several buildings in town, including a hidden cabinet in Buanna Cain's upstairs bathroom that I found by accident.

Buanna had plumbing problems and asked me to fix the pipes. While I was working on a leak in the upstairs bathroom, I somehow accidentally tripped a latch that caused the mirror to swing open. Behind the mirror was a concealed cabinet built into the wall. It contained a strange device with copper wires leading out to the roof. I looked out the window at the roof. There I saw what looked like a thick glass lens with a mirror that tilted on a swivel. The contraption pointed at the sky. I had no idea what I was looking at, but when I turned around, there stood Mrs. Cain. She had a look of rage, and I knew that she was upset that I had found her hidden device. When I left that day I observed a strange type of antennae on the roof near the chimney, visible from the backyard, but hidden from the street.'"

The agent continued. "He signed the letter at the bottom. Mr. Huber included a diagram of each of the alterations he had made to the city water pipes. This document will save the city hours in locating the menacing equipment. The letter was dated only a week before Mr. Huber turned up missing," the agent added.

"The Bureau sent a team to check Mrs. Cain's upstairs bathroom where they discovered the strange phone-type system. Our agents are trying to figure out how it works. They also found ledgers and other items they are scanning for further leads. We took the letter and the diagrams and confronted Buanna Cain with them just minutes ago," continued Steve. "We told her that the agents would soon uncover the depth of the damage she had caused our country, and she laughed! She was at her breaking point, perhaps, because suddenly she snapped! Our medic gave Mrs. Cain a relaxant, to keep her from having a heart attack, and as she began to calm down she said, with a crazed smile, I might add, 'It's too late! The information has already reached the Czorg! You cannot stop the zorgs! They have the means in an instant to put the major attack in motion. We have been planning this for years! The time is ripe. If it had not been for Annie Bigmouth, none of you would even be aware of what was happening to you! The zorgs will have signaled the other zorg networks located throughout the world, by now!' she said, laughing. 'I am sure the zorgs have sent a convoy to the Palace of the Great Czorg. He has his residence in a nearby province found beyond the nether world portal.'"

"We asked her what she was talking about and she said with a snide voice: 'Another world exists beyond this one. It occupies the same space but at a different vibration. Zorgs live in that otherworld but travel in and out of our world at will. Nothing but a thin curtain camouflages this separate world. You will never stop them!'"

"It seems that Mrs. Cain's reaction to the medication was to tell us everything she knows," said agent Steve. "She said there is a labyrinth of trails under the city that had been used for travel by zorgs for centuries. They escaped to alert their master of the disaster from the library room through this means. She said that the zorgs have an information system that volleys between the two worlds, bouncing messages off of the sun, which then projects the messages in to the other world," Steve said. "Her exact words were, 'I know this. I have one! You have found it! That darned machine was having a bad day. I could only hope my words went out on the rays. But it won't matter. The zorgs were all but ready when they were first discovered by the girl. I'm sure a zorg must have gotten word back to the Czorg, regardless.'" The agent almost perfectly imitated the crabby librarian's voice.

"Our specialists contacted the space lab. Increased sunspot activity has interfered with satellite receivers and television waves and may have also prevented the alerts to her accomplices from being delivered properly. We only hoped that the same laws of science apply to their equipment. So far, every person we contacted from Cain's phone list has been caught off-guard. I hope the zorg's communication system has problems, too.

"The Army is very much involved in the preparations for a planned assault in that dimension, if we find that it is feasible. We are working with a lens manufacturer in the area to secure as many prisms as available and to quickly create a prototype for a better lens our soldier can wear.

"The Army has also sent helicopters to different places throughout the country to collect moss for the antidote. We are pumping water from the nearby reservoir into several cow tanks and we then add the moss, salt, and the prism. The antidote 'cures' in the sunlight and then will be siphoned into five-gallon water jugs. A truckload of Sparklett's water jugs and their company truck will transport the antidote. The antidote can then be put into special fern sprayers with screens inserted, to insure no specks of the moss are allowed to clog the sprayers. We are developing a screen to cover each jug of water, as a further precaution. Massive quantities of salt have been ordered for the antidote."

"Going back to the subject of Mrs. Cain," the agent continued, "she said she wished she had been given the opportunity to call the other *humanz*, a name she assigned to all zorg sympathizers. The signal failure probably prevented any messages from getting through, because if they had, there would be a terrible outbreak of disease in the human race beginning already," the agent relayed. "She said that it was her own poor methods that allowed Annie out of her sight, and, unbelievably, the girl was able to find someone that had the 'Old Knowledge.' Mrs. Cain said she wished she had followed the girl home that day and gotten rid of her. She also said that if the officers had not caught her in the library that night she would have been able to discern that girl's pipe location and destroy her, and then none of the rest of the discoveries would have been made."

Chief Graham said, "Apparently she doesn't like Annie much." Everyone in the room laughed, albeit nervously. A little comic relief was just what they needed.

The agent on the telephone continued, "After remaining silent for only seconds, she blurted out, 'In fact, I should have just destroyed the book with the zorg information. It was library property, apparently donated ages past, so I was afraid to remove it from the shelves completely. What a blunder! I should have destroyed it completely, and taken the risk if it was discovered missing. Without that book, the girl may still have discovered the presence of zorgs, but the humans probably would not have so quickly discovered the antidote.'"

The agent added, "The interview was a stunning success after all, and headquarters has launched a search of the libraries across the country for more obscure information.

"The military is scrambling. As a precaution," Steve said, "the President of the United States has ordered the National Guard to send troops to occupy the defunct Minuteman nuclear bunkers. These soldiers will be separated from general society in case there is an attempt on our civilization. As a last resort, these combat troops will be isolated and able to respond independent of world circumstances. They have been instructed to wear the zorg goggles at all times. Missiles are currently being modified to hold the antidote for use against the zorgs."

"Normally the Center for Disease Control has techniques for destroying germs in a safe way, so that they are not re-introduced to the globe's water and air supplies. We are beginning to fear that we need to modify the normal method of destroying the germs, if the stockpile becomes too massive. That is all we have to report for now. Thank you all for your work in the field. We will keep you informed of further developments." He hung up.

    The men stood up to stretch their legs. It had seemed like a couple of hours since they had moved from their seats. John returned to his office. He dialed Augusta's phone number and left a message. He wished that she would answer the phone. It was getting late. She should be home by now.

Saturday, 4.11 p.m.

Neeze held the leather pouch close and tucked it tighter under his arm to protect it as he raced down the inner trail to Cell 56 on Floor Three in what the FBI guys called "The Big House." This federal prison housed the intended target, Mrs. Buanna Cain. Neeze hated this part of his job because the narrow air ducts made the going slow and miserable. When he was in a hurry, like he was today, the sharp metal ridges on the inner wall edges scraped the hairs right off anything that happened to be protruding as he rushed along. He already had three good scrapes and his hurrying hadn't gotten him anywhere that much faster. He had a deadline to meet, and his boss had threatened him with the loss of his life if he didn't intercept Buanna with a syringe full of poison before she had a chance to speak to the government team. It was imperative that she not tell the agents any of the information she had collected in her position as coordinator of her region.

Neeze's day went bad from the minute his office called him on his Saturday off and ordered him to poison Mrs. Cain. He needed to administer the injection before she was interrogated. The zorg network had identified where the prisoner had been sent earlier that day. The initial alert to Neeze's superiors had gone unanswered. Strangely, no zorgs had been on duty to receive the incoming message. By early afternoon, Neeze received word from his superiors that the woman in charge of the bungled operation had been arrested and was being sent to their district.

Neeze knew his victim. Her father had served the zorgs faithfully, as had her grandmother and other family members. Her husband had been a loose gun and he had died "mysteriously" several years ago in the state prison. That assignment had been given to Neeze's cousin, Glur. He lived near the portal by the state prison. His cousin especially enjoyed shooting Mr. Cain full of poison all those years ago after he threatened Buanna Cain with disclosure if she didn't get him out of prison on his theft and battery charges.

Only a small number of humans had been recruited over the centuries to help the zorg's operation, and this small number of people had proved to be risk-free up until now. Somehow the enemy had discovered the supplies warehoused in the workplace where this woman operated, and she'd been arrested before the problem could be corrected. Neeze's boss was terrified of the Czorg, knowing his own life was in peril, as well as Neeze's. The pressure was on Neeze to kill her before it was too late.

The zorgs seen by the police with Buanna before her arrest in the library wasted no time getting back to the portal near the hospital. They relayed the disastrous developments to the Czorg's palace during the wee hours of the night, causing all hell to break out on the nether side. Neeze couldn't help but find this to be a bit ironic, since the zorgs' intended goal had backfired on them. There was such panic! Many, many years had passed since the zorgs had encountered such a threat. Neeze knew he must make every second count.

He tiptoed along the final leg of the trip until he arrived at the right turn that led to the heat duct of Buanna Cain's cell. He peered in to see Buanna seated on a chair, surrounded by three FBI agents. He froze in place as fear overtook him. He was too late! She must have been here a long time before the superiors in Neeze's office knew about her arrival. She was acting drugged. She was smiling, which was very unusual, as she gave the men information regarding the ledger with the list of names and numbers for the *humanz* in the league and the zorgs' locations. She even told them about the communication system between worlds using the sun machine! The ledger she kept in the secret cabinet in the upstairs bathroom of her house also contained a log showing the best time to send messages. Neeze wondered if the humans would be able to interfere and possibly intercept zorg communications with this log.

Neeze looked down on the woman below and listened as Buanna told the agents everything she knew!

Neeze looked down on the woman below and listened as Buanna told the agents everything she knew! He heard her tell the FBI agents that she had tried to send an alert to the Czorg Palace warning them about the girl the very first day, but the sunspot activity had been wrong and the energy necessary to direct the message was insufficient. The local zorgs would have long ago warned the Czorg of the unfolding situation through their daily contacts. She planned to send messages to alert the other regional directors, *humanz* involved with the zorgs, but she never got the chance. Instead, first she tried to do damage control on her own by calling on the local zorgs to help her locate the girl's plumbing route in order to infect her family with salmonella, a fast acting bacterium, to keep the girl in bed and her mouth shut. "If she had only brought a flashlight instead of turning on the library light, the girl would now likely be dead," the librarian confided to the agents.

Not knowing what the woman would say next made Neeze feel nauseated. He tried to decide what to do. The woman had already told the men the most damaging information. Was there more that she hadn't yet said? Should he use the syringe on her or just let it go, since he was too late to stop her from giving the enemy the important knowledge? He leaned back into the air duct, feeling sick throughout his entire body. Fear was a terrible feeling to deal with. The thought crossed his mind that maybe he should poison himself. Voices drifted into the air duct from Buanna's jail cell, bringing him out of his deep thought. He heard the officers ask to be let out of the cell. The clank of steel against steel echoed through that section of the prison as the jailer opened, then closed, the metal door.

Neeze decided to go back, report to his superiors what had happened, and then find out if he should kill the woman anyway. It wouldn't help much to kill her now. He started back to the local quarters, taking his time. Neeze wasn't in a big hurry to go back to his boss to tell him the bad news. He was scared that they would be mad at him for not getting to the cell to kill the woman before she could talk. He had tried to get there! It was their fault they got the message to him too late! Everything was spinning out of control so fast!

Neeze limped back to his station and dreaded the rest of his day. Neeze had at least three wide scrapes on his elbows and one on his knee. The blood was matted and sticky. He was not happy. He had been around long enough to know that when bad things happened in his world, the powerful zorgs vented their anger on anyone, human or zorg. Neeze knew that he, a working class zorg, would probably have a very bad day, a very bad day indeed.

Saturday, 5:35 p.m.

Zagar held himself close to the tree, hiding. He had been following the intruders as they advanced through the trees towards the clearing. He was grateful Magnus had spent his time talking to the humans. It helped to cover any sounds he made trying to stay hidden in the brush. It was strange how the humans had made so much progress against the zorgs in such a short time period. The zorgs' efforts to help Mrs. Cain launch the germs against the one they called Annie had been prevented by the police. When the cops discovered Buanna Cain and some zorgs in the Library Launch Center, it was a major blow to the Zorg Organization, or, as the lesser zorgs often referred to it, the Zorg Org. Zagar jokingly referred to himself as a worker of the drone zone, and his pals laughed at his clever turn of the language. Magnus's voice drifted through the trees again, and the exhausted zorg snapped back to attention.

The zorgs had been discovered by a snit of a girl. Of all the humans that he might have solicited to gain a little extra zip that day, curse Mozag for trying to absorb Annie's essence! He could have saved the entire clan all of these problems if the girl hadn't seen him in the reflection of the glass. Mrs. Cain didn't handle the girl very well, either. Her sloppy library methods left such an important book out in the public domain. What a mistake! How one insignificant event could undo years of effort in a few hours boggled Zagar's evil little brain.

Zagar received word hours ago that the police confiscated another significant stash of disease vials from the home of Mrs. Cain at noon. Why had the zorgs put all their stockpiles for that city in only two locations? Zagar shook his head at the incompetency of his peers. The zorg communities all over the world would be in jeopardy if these local boys did not get a grip!

Zagar's fears increased as he glimpsed an image of his future in a fiery pit. Somehow he and the others must stop this chain of events. He thought about when he was a little lad. He had asked his father why the zorgs stayed on the side of the devil if the devil was going to lose eventually. His dad told him that the statement was made by God to throw the zorgs off balance. He insisted it was a ploy to diminish the zorgs' courage in their battle against Him. Zorgs believed themselves to be God's equal, as does the devil. Their arrogance is bolstered by Lucifer's weekly newsletters. The 'Mission Statement' is printed in bold type at the bottom of each edition encouraging the zorgs to tear the fabric of society as wide as possible to ensure that "to the zorgs go the spoils." Now Zagar wondered if the zorgs had bet on a bad horse and that they would all have to pay dearly at the ticket counter.

He had been assigned to watch the elven portal for further developments. This alliance of the elves with the humans might cripple the zorgs battle strategy completely. Zagar was especially worried ever since he heard the conversation between the lady and Magnus. The humans knew about the antidote! What could go wrong next? His leaders would be even angrier to find that someone with the "Old Knowledge" was helping the investigation. This really depressed him. The zorgs had gone from living in obscurity in the human realm to being sought by law enforcement agencies in less than two days! His head hurt. He was tired from being up all day and all night with the rest of the zorg community.

He followed the five figures making their way towards the castle. Magnus's voice became muffled through the brush ahead. When Zagar emerged on the path, he was face to face with a growling dog, crouched and ready for an attack. Zagar fled up the tree trunk nearest him, gripping with his long claws, then tried to find a path along the branches high above the ground. He needed to hide before any stinking birds came to the dog's aid. Zagar was not in the mood! He tore one of his claws in the bark on the ancient tree. For someone that enjoyed others' pain, he found that he did not enjoy pain for himself at all.

Saturday, 5:53 p.m.

John couldn't stand waiting in the office. It had been hours, with four messages on Ms. Nichols answering machine. Where were they? Chief Graham called the patrol watching Augusta's neighborhood. No activity had been spotted in either of the houses that the officers were guarding. John felt worthless just sitting around, so he drove first to Augusta's house. He stopped to check in with the patrol unit guarding the neighborhood first. They reported no new developments. He pulled into Augusta's driveway.. He could see no sign of them. He got out of the cruiser, then walked through Michelle's yard and circled around to Augusta's back porch. Rapping several times at the door, he tried the handle. Twisting it open easily, John went inside. A muscular cat with a prism on its collar met him and meowed, then rubbed his side along the Chief's pant leg. John bent down and scratched him behind the ears. The cat purred loudly. John decided to do a check of the place before leaving.

Walking through the little laundry room and sink area, John entered the kitchen where two parrots began chattering. The noise startled John because he heard the birds before seeing them. John picked up the friendly cat and they both looked on at the parrots.

"Pretty Kitty! Who's your friend?" one of the birds asked. John smiled to himself. As a youngster, John spent many hours at the zoo in his hometown. He loved the aviary, and especially liked the parrots and cockatoos.

"I wonder how old they are," John thought to himself, mentally noting that parrots can live for eighty years or more.

"Pretty Birds!" John responded to the duo, and after another few seconds, he continued circling through the house. Clearly the girls and Augusta were not here. Worry nagged at John's normally steady demeanor. Was something wrong? Where were they? As he left, he took the cat with him. Maybe this feline could be of some use.

John placed the cat in the police cruiser, started it up, and backed out of the driveway. He headed north out of town where Augusta said they would be. He scanned the roadside for the telltale gate Augusta described this morning in her conversation. There it was! A gate stood open and he drove down the winding dirt road at the north edge of a cornfield. To the left were a pasture and a winding slough that held a couple of small ponds. Cattle grazed lazily in the pasture beyond the fence and watched him as he drove past.

He wound his way eastward towards the river. The road took a dip to the left through some trees and opened to a grassy clearing on the other side. John saw a vehicle parked in the little meadow-could it be Augusta's? The high land here overlooked the river and creek bed. A cabin stood visible through the trees. The Chief parked next to the car and turned his cruiser off. The cat stood on the front seat and looked through the window at the other car. He meowed, like he was calling Augusta. John got out. Peering through the car window, he saw supplies on the front seat. He didn't notice any signs of a problem. He opened Augusta's car door and looked through the supplies. A jug with moss and some other things were on the seat. He shut the car door. He went back to the police car and retrieved Augusta's cat. On the picnic table nearby there were four jars of water with specks, probably the moss, and a prism in each container. Zorg antidote! Great! It had been in the sun, hopefully, already for an hour.

The purring cat, prism dangling, was enjoying this trip with John. He noted how well behaved the cat was. With Tiggy under his arm, he walked back to the cop car and grabbed a fern sprayer off the front seat that he thoughtfully brought along. He went back to the picnic table and set the cat down. He unscrewed the lids to both the fern sprayer and one of the jars of antidote. After removing the prism, he placed a handkerchief over the mouth of the quart jar and poured the liquid slowly into the fern sprayer. He hoped the cloth might keep the sprayer nozzle clear of any loose particles of moss. The cat sat patiently, watching his every move, as though waiting for the adventure to begin.

John radioed headquarters and reported the location of Ms. Nichol's car, but the whereabouts of the four were still unknown. He informed the answering officer of the antidote and told him to send a unit out to get a supply for the police team and the FBI right away.

Saturday, 5:59 p.m.

The FBI organized a team to locate and detain every person that could be identified from Buanna Cain's phone records. These phone records were one of the few ways to collect more information on this complex and mysterious case. The Bureau needed to know more about these *humanz*, and were trying to locate as many of them as possible. Hopefully, new interrogation techniques approved by the Patriot Act would be useful if the suspects refused to cooperate.

The phone records betrayed people from all walks of life. Some even held official positions in government, the armed services, and prisons. Within a few hours, sixty percent of the phone calls had been traced and these people brought into custody. In luck, all of the *humanz* detained so far had been caught unaware. It was the job of the FBI to keep the operation as secret as possible. Each residence was searched thoroughly to retrieve their answering machines, cell phones, and any suspicious items. More of the strange sun machines and vials of communicable disease had been found in many of these homes. So much poison had been found already that the Center for Disease Control had decided that the shipments of germs in the United States should all be put into one stockpile near Nevada, where miners had emptied uranium deposits. These empty mines, huge holes in the ground, would be the perfect place to dump the contamination.

FBI agent Pete Jacobs, tired and worn out, spoke to the large group of men and women seated in the conference room. "Men, ladies, it is hard to believe that we discovered this threat only a day or so ago. Never before have our agents been expected to achieve so much to save the lives of the citizens of our country and even the world. You all deserve a big pat on the back. Our men and women in the field have done an excellent job locating these zorg cohorts. We suspect that there are more out there. "We need to start searching through prisons and the slums and other likely places that we haven't thought to look. These people might not have steady lives but they too may also work for the zorgs on the streets and in the jails. Thankfully, *humanz* are easily identified by their zorg tattoo.

Agent Jacobs held up his pair of prism glasses and smiled. "The main complaint from the field is the fact that these prism glasses are cumbersome and difficult to adjust when using them for regular sight and then switching to the prism-mode to see zorgs. Oh, yeah-and more than one guy has complained that these glasses look ridiculous!" He smiled.

Saturday, 6:05 p.m.

All three girls trailed behind Augusta and Magnus as the group wound around the last of the trail before they reached the drawbridge to the castle. Augusta felt like she had been reunited with an old friend as she visited with Magnus. They made their way through the trees. Magnus told Augusta, "Several years ago the elves realized that the zorgs were getting larger and the cats in our world were having trouble fighting the ugly beasts. The elves needed a bigger-sized cat to prowl the realm. The elves came up with the idea to get some earth cats because they are so much larger." Magnus explained, "The cats we have here now are likely related to the two cats that my older brother, Oliver, found as kittens in the woods along the river of your family farm long ago. They had been abandoned by a passing motorist along the bridge near the woods. Oliver brought the kittens back through the portal many years ago. By now, all of our castle cats are related, I'm sure. The human cats just boosted the average size of the cats here with their bloodline. The two new cats liked living in our dimension. I think they might have had a pretty hard life where they were abandoned. Lucky for us, though."

Magnus described the first cat as a strong male with a brown and gold tiger striped coat, named Rocky. "Rocky has been the king of the castle since he arrived all those years ago." Magnus said. "Aging is slower in our world. Rocky is still alive, but his strength is waning. He is still able to kill a zorg in one slash, though. Libby was the name of the other cat Oliver brought home that day. She was the most beautiful cat in the realm. Her fur was pure white with faint light gray stripes, and black tips on her ears and nose and tail. Her eyes were bright light blue. She glowed with health. She had several litters after she came to us, although she passed away about five years ago when she was somehow poisoned by the zorgs."

The group continued on a path of flat smooth stones. They arrived at the entrance to the castle. It was secured by a wrought iron gate. A tall ivy-covered iron fence surrounded the castle grounds. Once the visitors arrived, Magnus reached up and pulled strongly on the thick rope attached to a large bell in a tower above. It chimed noisily. A guard appeared in the tower window within seconds and smiled down on the new arrivals. "We've been waiting for you, Magnus! Pleased to meet you, ladies!" the elf called to the human visitors. The sound of a chain clanked and the bridge began to lower.

Magnus led the group across the bridge to the main door, which suddenly opened to expose a throng of elves gathered to meet the very first people ever to come to visit their castle. Magnus gleamed with pride as he introduced the newcomers to Linda, his lovely wife. Linda gracefully bowed to them and welcomed the visitors to their castle. Magnus introduced the group to the waiting elves. The girls shook hands with their new friends.

Magnus told the crowd of elves that he met the group as they collected moss for the zorg antidote next to the Battle Fork portal. Annie felt like she belonged in a storybook. The elves looked like characters from a Disney movie. Their faces glowed and their demeanor was cordial. Above the conversations, Magnus asked for everyone's attention. He asked the group to follow him into the main conference hall. It reminded Annie of student assemblies in her school gym. The elves were excited as they took their seats. Annie felt the stare of elves following the group as Magnus, Augusta, Annie, Maggie, and Michelle were escorted to a front table by the elders.

Magnus announced, "Fellow elves, I am so pleased to welcome our visitors today. We have been battling the zorgs diligently throughout the ages, and now the human help that was prophesied long ago has arrived in the form of this unassuming group. We do know that the Lord works in mysterious ways." Annie saw smiles across all the elf faces.

Magnus turned to Annie and her friends. "You have discovered the importance of our work after seeing the zorgs in your own world. Up until today, no human has actually been to our castle, nor have any entered the portal to this world although, as I told you, years back we acquired the felines Libby and Rocky to assist us in this battle.

"It is written in elven lore, that in the end times, zorgs will directly influence worldly governments. At that time the humans and elves-men will unite against the zorgs. I met this group today as they collected moss for the zorg antidote near the Battle Fork portal. At about 3 p.m. today, on my daily scout mission, I spotted Annie. She was able to see me clearly without her prism glasses. She introduced me to Augusta, Maggie, and Michelle. They told me that they were preparing a zorg antidote and immediately I knew that the "Great Breach" must have occurred, as prophesied long ago.

"I told these girls how the zorgs plan to switch their *humanz* with the true leaders, sure to be attempted soon. Events on the earth are reaching a peak, as described in the Holy Bible's book of Revelations. One of the most certain details of this time frame delineates that the end time would arrive within one generation of Israel becoming a nation. It may very well have already begun. As further prophesied, this tribulation will culminate in a face-off between the second coming of Jesus Christ and the Antichrist, already upon the earth and preparing his grand entrance soon.

Magnus smiled at his captivated audience, fascinated by the unfolding events. "Thankfully, Annie was injured in an accident.

Sorry Annie for the way that must sound-" Magnus turned and smiled at Annie. "Causing that injury was the initial zorg mistake. The injury made her eyes to tear-up and she spotted the very zorg that we believe caused the girl's accident, in a reflection in the storefront window where she knelt. What is even stranger is the fact that because of this zorg sighting, Maggie introduced Annie to Augusta, her cousin Michelle's neighbor, who had knowledge of the zorgs.

A loud bell clamored. Annie saw a worried look cross Magnus's face. Two elves had just entered the great hall. Magnus crossed the room to speak with them. The older of the two, an army-clad elf, spoke with Magnus and several elders that also joined them. They spoke for minutes before Magnus escorted the soldier to where Augusta and the girls sat. He introduced the visitors to Scoggins, the elder elf and military leader. "Scoggins came to report that a throng of zorgs have been spotted traveling en masse near our castle," Magnus explained. "You and your companions may not be safe here. I will guide you safely back to the entrance portal to your world. We anticipate a zorg battle soon."

Saturday, 6:29 p.m.

John held the purring cat and headed north through the trees. He wore his prism glasses as he made his way on the slight trail. He had called for the missing party, and searched the banks and trees to the south of the cabin area before finding tracks and evidence of foot traffic through the woods to the north. The sky was still blue and sunny. Daylight savings time in the middle of summer left plenty of daylight, giving him more time to find the missing girls. A breeze wisped through the high branches. Following the trail he came to a giant cottonwood tree. There was a trampling of the ground and the trail seemed to stop. He circled the tree. The base of the tree was huge, almost eight feet in diameter. "Wow!" John thought to himself. "I didn't know cottonwood trees could get that big." Huge gnarled branches scraped the sky high above, and a cleft ran down one side of its trunk. Looking closer, John saw something shiny on the ground near the trunk. He reached down and picked it up. John instantly recognized Maggie's watch. It was the watch Maggie showed him that morning when she described how she met Augusta. But after looking around and yelling for the group, the watch proved a poor consolation prize. "Where are they?!" John exclaimed aloud. Fear started creeping in on his thoughts. "I hope they are okay," he thought. "But the wooded area is not that big. If they were anywhere nearby, they would hear my call. Why would Augusta abandon her car like that? Trying to decide if he should call in a search team and contact the girl's parents, he leaned against the tree. He fell through the solid tree, and caught his balance in time to be startled by an equally astonished elf.

Shaking his head and rubbing his eyes, Chief Graham looked at the elf. He could see him without his prism glasses as well. Partly bewildered but also partly amused, Chief Graham pocketed his prism glasses and introduced himself, extending his hand to the small soldier. John held the curious cat slightly forward and told the elf that the cat belonged to a woman named Augusta, and that he was searching for her and three teenage girls.

Gary introduced himself and saluted Chief Graham. "I am so glad to meet you, Chief. I heard about you from Augusta and her companions. Your friends were here today. They went with Magnus to the castle, but I am beginning to worry. They should have returned to this portal by now. I sent a dispatch pigeon to tell the elders at the castle that Augusta and the girls have not returned. A zorg-elf battle is brewing, and we wanted Augusta and the girls safely back through the portal before the battle began."

John stomach tightened. Augusta and the girls might be in the hands of the zorgs right now! "What do I need to know about this place before I begin searching for the girls?"

"The events following Annie's discovery have created panic among the zorg population. Any help the human race brings to this realm is very welcome, but it has to be natural. No machinery that operates on electricity or processed petroleum fuels will work in this dimension. However, things like gravity, fire and wind are exactly the same as the human realm."

John tried to turn on his flashlight. It would not work. Weird! John asked the soldier elf if he thought a glider or air balloon, like a blimp, would work in this world. "I believe a glider would work well in our world, and we often have wind enough to operate one," the elf noted. "As far as a blimp, however, I believe that the gas used to float the blimp would be considered unnatural to this world."

"Up until Annie's discovery, the animals have been our biggest allies. The birds send us telepathic views from their vantage points. Dogs and cats also help patrol and protect our castles and portals. Cats are the number one zorg killers. Perhaps the cat you are carrying will be helpful.

"You must also know that in this world, zorgs know the power of God and are unable to snatch those in His hand. Those that come to help us in the battle here must be clean of heart, and followers of truth. One last note-a prism isn't needed to see the zorgs in this dimension, but a prism wipes out the zorgs' energy. We think it's the symbolism of the triangle that the prism represents."

Gary continued and asked John, "Is that a radio you have on your shoulder? It is also useless here. Before you go to look for your friends, alert the rest of your agency of your agenda and how they can prepare. You will need reinforcements. Your missing friends will probably require a lot more help. They might be standing trial before the Czorg right now. Please hurry!"

John thanked his new friend. "May I leave the cat with you?"

"Of course! Godspeed," he emphasized. "I'll send a message right now telling the elders that human reinforcements are on the way. Perhaps we can hold the zorgs at bay."

John held the cat and waited while Gary wrote and then placed the handwritten note into a leather pouch. Gary reached into the aviary and a bird landed on his extended index finger. He fastened the little pouch to the bird's leg and released the bird with a swift gesture towards the skies.

Gary took Tiggy from John's arms and directed the soldier to stand where he would automatically shift to the other portal. In a flash, John was back in the woods north of town, at the same place he'd been standing earlier. He pressed the button on his flashlight. It was working perfectly again. He pressed the radio button by his collar. The dispatcher came on immediately. "Patch this message to the FBI and my officers." John waited while the radio operator complied. As John stood there, he looked up at the sky. The sun was lower in the western sky. The radio cracked and the dispatcher announced that the parties had been contacted and were on the line. "We need help, NOW, at the north edge of town…"

Saturday, 6:42 p.m.

Zagar and Neeze looked down from the thick branches at Magnus and another elf talking to the group of humans they had been leading through the trees. Magnus was guiding the group along the path back to the portal. The spying zorgs heard every word that Magnus said as they made their way along.

"Maybe next time we can have a nice meal and show you a little 'small folk' hospitality. I suppose it is getting late anyway, and we didn't really plan for you to be here long. I'm just sorry that you had to leave so quickly, before we barely caught our breath."

Once the travelers left the trees, the two zorgs had to scramble to keep up with them. Running parallel to the trail, they leaped at times from rock to rock. Their claws were sore from the constant travel that day, and jumping on rocks and grabbing the tree branches only made their bodies hurt worse.

This was Neeze's and Zagar's last chance to keep from failing their Czorg. Almost to the entrance to the portal now, a few trees dotted the cliff side of the trail, and the zorgs were able to leap from limb to limb, following the entourage closely.

Magnus, his companion and the returning humans trekked as quickly as they could back towards the portal. With twenty yards to go, the group heard urgent yells coming from the direction of the castle and two sounds very similar to gunshots. Magnus turned to look back in that direction, worry spreading across his face.

He pointed to the portal entrance, a short distance ahead. "Continue on the trail a few yards or so to the portal entrance back to your world. I'm sorry ladies, but an emergency requires our attention. Move as quickly as you can the rest of the way. Gary or Andy or one of the other sentries will assist you. Thank you so much for all of your help. I hope to see you soon!" Magnus gave them a quick hug before he and his companion ran back towards the castle.

The zorgs leaped ahead and waited, looking down as the group below hurried toward the portal. Neeze and Zagar glanced sideways at each other and smiled. "Finally some good luck has come our way," Neeze whispered to Zagar. Just below the spot where the zorgs hid in their branches, the trail narrowed and thistles grew close to large rocks, forming a bottleneck. It was the best place to strike an ambush. Both zorgs had loaded their nose syringes, like weapons, as they had been instructed to inject the humans only if they tried to escape. The Czorg was waiting at the palace to interview the people and wanted them alive. Neeze narrowly escaped death that very afternoon when he'd failed to reach Cain before she talked. He pleaded for another chance to avenge the zorgs' (and his own) plight.

Hours ago Zagar had given the Czorg a full report of the latest development. After he fled the dog attack, he reported to his superiors that the intruders were actually here on the zorgs' home soil. The Czorg was furious to learn that the humans had been allowed to enter this realm. How did this happen? Who was responsible? The Czorg knew very well that this situation had been prophesied-but he had spent way too many hours preparing against this very event-could it possibly be true? Humans must not occupy this realm! This would indicate the end times and the Czorg's certain doom!

The Czorg needed damage control at any cost. Neeze, in a last chance effort to spare his own life, was directed to capture the females that had entered the portal before they were able to return to earth with damaging information.

Zagar dropped between the girls and Augusta, abruptly halting their progress along the trail. The people gasped at the sudden attack! Stealthily, Augusta dropped the gunny sack she had been holding under a low hanging branch nearby. In this dimension, Augusta, Annie, Michelle and Maggie could see and smell the zorgs clearly. Michelle and Maggie started to gag.

Neeze lunged from his perch towards Annie, who happened to be the last of the troop walking single file on the narrow path. Neeze's bloody knuckles gripped her wrist, as he prepared to inject his nose syringe filled with a yellowish brown liquid. "Cooperate or die!" he spoke in guttural English.

All four captives put their hands over their heads in surrender. Zagar ordered the people to march through a disguised opening to the side of the bottlenecked path, up a slight incline through the trees. Seeing the zorgs' sharp needle noses dripping with poison, they followed the orders being barked at them. They formed a line and began to walk in single file behind the leading zorg. The other zorg followed behind. There was no path. After traveling through the brush for maybe half of an hour, the frightened visitors and their captors finally reached a dark stone path leading to a black palace nestled in the tall shadowy trees at the edge of the Nether Glen.

Four more zorgs suddenly appeared when the troop drew near. The prisoners were herded through the back gate. Immediately, Annie was separated from the others. The woman and the other two girls were led down a dark hallway to a guard post. The zorgs bound them and placed them together in a cell with four cots. The frightened captives sat on the cots in the dank room. The sounds of dripping water kept a monotonous beat somewhere in the dark cell. Occasionally the sounds of footsteps added to the beat. They heard the raspy voices of zorgs from somewhere nearby, and the faint sound of Annie's voice. "The zorgs separated Annie first, so that they could interview her," Augusta said to the girls.

Augusta kept her head between her knees, fighting nausea. Maggie and Michelle kept trying to loosen their bounds as best as they could. The group took comfort in each other's company, talking quietly among themselves. They were worried about Annie. They were afraid they might be overheard. Augusta suggested that they say the Lord's Prayer. "Remember, it can only help." She whispered, "Concentrate on Annie while you pray."

Saturday, 6:43 p.m.

Gary met him when John re-entered the portal only minutes after he had radioed the new information back to his headquarters and the FBI. There was still daylight to work with. John picked up the cat once again, ready to begin the search. Gary escorted the soldier down the trail a short way, pointing out the distant castle and the direction from which the travelers were returning. Gary wished John luck as John headed down the trail. After traveling a short distance, John noticed scuffles in the dirt path. He looked around. When he looked up, he spotted a broken branch and ruffled leaves. His law enforcement instinct told him that this was the scene of a crime. He began searching the surrounding terrain and saw the gunnysack slumped under the branches of a tree near the trail. Picking it up, he saw that it contained a bag with the prism glasses and a jug of water. Augusta and the girls had been here! John put the bag back in its hiding place. Setting the big cat down for a second, he separated the branches, There was evidence of recent travel through this spot. It could have been caused by several persons passing this way. He picked up the cat again after first readjusting his bag. They were on their way.

He began tracking the path that the group had made through the brush. Deeper into the trees he went, continually finding a broken branch or smashed foliage to guide his way. The growth here was plush. The environment was unlike that on the other side of the portal. Everything, whether the sky, the trees, the dirt, it all seemed more vibrant. The countryside resembled John's impression of what the Garden of Eden must have looked like.

Overhead, a bird circled high above the valley east of his position. He sensed the bird was trying to show him something. He concentrated on the circling bird. Suddenly, Chief Graham spotted marauding zorgs some distance ahead in his mind's eye. They were having some celebratory pep rally of sorts. John intuited the movement of a group beyond that. Two zorgs were escorting a group of humans through a gate of a black palace. Concentrating, he could see Augusta and the three girls!

Memorizing the scene, he visualized the trail to his destination before the image faded. John felt relief. He now knew they were alive and, hopefully, he could get them released and back to safety very soon. He whispered to the cat still nestled in his arms that he had just spotted Augusta and the girls. He crept along the recent path. He was trying to hurry now. It was slow moving, traveling through such heavy growth.

He whispered to the cat still nestled in his arms
that he had just spotted Augusta and the girls.

Saturday, 7:11 p.m.

Zagar and Neeze had met the Czorg's ultimatum by capturing the intruding humans. They took the captives to the palace. Zagar was certain they would soon be interrogated. The zorgs weren't happy, though, when the Czorg wouldn't let them off the hook. He ordered them both to return immediately, before they even got a break, to guard the trail near the portal the four females used. The Czorg blamed Neeze for the sloppy timing that cost him the opportunity to get rid of that dumb woman, Buanna Cain, before she could be interrogated.

The Czorg commanded that they guard the incoming trail to prevent others from following the tracks made when the zorgs captured the girls. "You better be able to guard this position!" the Czorg had warned.

The two exhausted zorgs waited up above in the trees, sleepily watching for any intruders. It would be getting dark soon, and it would be a long, long night. Neither one of the drones had gotten a wink of sleep since the news of the previous night from the library reached the ears of the Czorg.

Not long after the two fumbling zorgs found their positions in the trees, the sound of rustling leaves attracted their attention. They watched the path below them intently. No matter how tired they were, they had enough sense to bring along a package of netting! The zorgs wove nets for use during battles. Nets could stop just about anything: big dogs, cats, and elves.

Zagar and Neeze placed the net into position. Their work being done, they decided to rest a little while they stood guard. They had been at this new post for just minutes it seemed, when a muscular-looking, uniformed human crept along the path below them. Zagar and Neeze, as if in one movement, untied the net strings, and the circular fabric dropped over the man below. He tried to duck around the trap, but it was too late. "Drat, something escaped!" Zagar exclaimed. From the corner of his eye, Zagar caught the movement. The sun was three quarters of an hour from setting, but even in the darkening woods there was still plenty of light to see the scampering cat. It must have been traveling with this man.

It only took the zorgs a few moments to jump from their treetop perch and secure the net. John had learned during jungle warfare training twenty years ago not to squirm if netted. He tried to remain calm, but his stress level made it hard not to thrash about in an attempt to escape. He released the cat before the net made it all the way to the ground. John hoped that the cat wasn't standing around waiting for him, or the foul zorgs might try to capture Augusta's cat, too. "Yuk!" John let out. John could smell the nasty zorgs as they busied themselves cinching the net tighter around him. His best bet was to cooperate rather than make matters worse. He still had the use of his hands, and if he was slow about it, he might be able to get to his antidote without them noticing, and get these two before they got the chance to bring in reinforcements.

Neeze and Zagar were too foggy in their thinking to realize that this man was more than they could handle. The prism held in the soldier's pocket was working against the zorgs' already sloppy thinking process. Zagar threw a strap over the tangled man's legs to his companion, who was waiting. John slid his hand stealthily to his spray bottle, located in the bag slung over his shoulder and resting under his left arm. He reached through the canvas opening and was prepared when both zorgs' smelly faces were near him in the finishing-up stage of securing their enemy. He held the spray bottle to the net and sent a quick shot of the poison into both faces in one movement. Within seconds, the two zorgs were writhing in the foliage, bubbles coming from their needle noses. The stench gagged the seasoned soldier.

"Great!" thought John. He was free to go now, except that he was hogtied. With some difficulty, he tried to extend his hand to the pant pocket holding his switchblade knife. The netting was tight, making it impossible. John listened intently for zorg activity in the area. His fingers began working for release from this trap. "Patience, patience," John reminded himself as his fingers got busy with the tedious task at hand.

Saturday, 7:13 p.m.

Tiggy leapt from the man's arms just before that thing tried to catch him. He scampered up the nearest tree and looked down on the group as the two rat things bent over the man with a net. Tiggy was tempted to leap down on them, but wasn't sure what they were. He knew that they were bad. The man was totally wrapped up now.

Tiggy crept along the tree branches and jumped to the next tree. As he traveled high above the ground, his prism caught a glimmer of the sunlight lowering off to the west. Tiggy found a good place to go back to the ground and scampered down. He could smell his master's scent and knew the woman had been this way. Maybe if he could just find her, she could help him get his new friend out of trouble back there. Tiggy followed the trail, a small figure making his way along. His little form cast a long shadow from the brilliant golden setting sunlight that penetrated the woods.

The trail wound on and on. Tiggy, unconcerned about time, didn't worry about it. Finally, the trail turned to dirt and then to an actual path. Not quite sure of where he was, and a little frightened by this whole adventure thing, the cat strayed off the main trail, following at a parallel. After awhile, Tiggy saw the shape of a big building. It looked uninviting. He could still smell his master's scent, though, and followed it toward the scary building.

Tiggy saw some more of the big rats in a group walking towards him up ahead in the growing moonlight. He ducked until they passed. He hoped that they wouldn't be able to smell him, though he could sure smell them. It was a smell worse than any dog he'd ever met.

Once they were gone, the muscular striped cat headed back to the trail. The trail bottlenecked and then opened out and a distinct path led to a bridge. He ran as fast as possible across the wooden bridge and then followed the trail as it turned left for a little bit before it straightened out. In the darkening sky Tiggy could see the big black palace directly ahead.

Tiggy stood in the shadows watching the place and saw a rat walk around the corner. He waited and the rat-thing came back around again a little bit later. The cat waited longer, observing the big structure, and sure enough, the rat-thing came back again. "This thing just goes in circles!" the cat noted.

The next time the patrol zorg passed by, the cat leapt into action and ran directly through the open uninviting black doorway. He headed down a dark corridor. Tiggy sensed danger. He could smell the scent of his beloved master even though the palace held the stench of zorg. In his mind he saw a huge place where the giant rats were gathered. He could feel the sickening energy emanating from that direction down the hallway. He wandered that way, keeping his nose down for the traces of his master.

Saturday, 7:30 p.m.

Bile and Gaul hid behind the grill of the return air duct to the kitchen in the old police station. They had been instructed to sever the natural gas line somewhere in the building. Bile hoped for a gas stove in the kitchen and decided to look there first. What was a relatively simple job two days ago was now incredibly tricky. It seemed every officer in the building was wearing those dumb prism glasses. Bile could tell the stress was getting to more than a few of them, too, because several officers kept returning to the kitchen to grab yet another snack off the table. The constant foot traffic made Bile uneasy. The simple life of the zorg was no more. Only two days ago, they could roam the earth as they pleased, in obscurity. The girl had changed all of that.

The original zorg plan had been so simple. At the appointed time, zorgs intended to infect the human population with so many serious viruses at one time that "normal" life would be completely disrupted. With so many governmental seats vacated, humanz (having vaccinated themselves over a period of time from these diseases) would gracefully fill necessary governmental roles and "save the day." Having *humanz* in control would pave the way for complete zorg control of the world.

That plan was but a memory now, it seemed. Bile creeped through the vent's grill and examined the layout of the room from his position on the floor. A microwave was plugged into the wall on the counter. Bile's wish to see a gas line had been crushed. "How are we going to get this building to explode?" he thought. If the police had cooked in this little kitchen before the invention of the microwave oven, it must have been with a hotplate. There wasn't any room for a stove in the room.

This would make their job even harder. Now they would need to travel back through the air duct to the furnace. Perhaps there was a place where they could open a valve off of the furnace line. They needed to eliminate the men that worked out of this office. Lots of FBI and CDC agents scurried about, making this worn-down building a regional headquarters.

Neither zorg wanted to be the one to report back to the Czorg without successfully completing their mission. They lifted the grate and entered the kitchen vent and began scampering along its route from the kitchen, hoping that further down the line they would find the furnace room. They crept along the air ducts and found the route to somewhere in the guts of the basement below. They dropped to the floor through an opening in the metal shaft. Both zorgs felt comfortable in the dank and dingy place. They began searching for the furnace.

Bile realized that they had emerged from a central air conditioning unit. "Dang! Wasn't there a furnace also connected to the system?" Bile asked Gaul. They could find no furnace connected to the air ducts, so that must mean that any heating unit in the old station must be electric base boards. The two decided to look for the water heater. "Perhaps, with luck, it was heated with gas," each thought. They located a water heater and found the plug for its electric heating unit.

Gaul volunteered to go back upstairs and look for the source of heat in the station above. Maybe there was another system that was piped in from the outside right into the first floor. He started back upstairs. Bile decided to follow, since there was no good reason for him to wait below. They both slipped back into the duct and followed the tracks in the dust they had made earlier. They rounded a corner.

Gaul peeked through the register vent to see what kind of heating system they might find as they attempted to search the rooms on the ground floor. Bile went around him to check the next opening.

Bile gasped when he got to the next register vent. "Look there!" he said to his partner. Below him Bile saw a box of the poisonous vials on a desk. It was one of the several stockpiled wooden crates so painstakingly filled with the nose syringe-sized vials over the course of his lifetime and even longer. Now it was little more than wasted effort! Bile's distaste of Annie grew by the minute. Bile turned back to call again to Gaul. Gaul was not behind him! Gaul must not have followed him. He must have gone out the register back into the kitchen.

Bile wanted to continue his search. He approached the final room at the end of the steel corridor. Suddenly he heard the exclamation, "A zorg!" A loud clanking sound immediately followed. Sick in the very pit of his stomach, Bile got even sicker when he crept back to the kitchen. Through the vent register, Bile could see three men wearing their prism glasses standing over poor Gaul. Gaul had been caught! Bile could see the heavy salt shaker lying near Gaul's bloody head. Gaul looked up at the human faces and he wished he could escape their view. The last thing he saw before he began to fade out of consciousness was an electric baseboard heater installed along the floor. Gaul pointed to the heater and wanted to ask the men if that was the only source of heat for the office. He never had the chance. His buddy watched through the register only feet from where the zorg slipped into a coma.

Bile turned and scampered back down the steel corridor. He stealthily made his way from the police headquarters back outside. As a final effort to find the police building's source of heat, Bile checked through three windows from the outside. He saw electric baseboard heaters along the walls of the rooms he checked, which were impossible to see from his vantage point in the air ducts earlier. There was no gas to the building.

In the nearing twilight, Bile raced along the curb, hoping no officers wearing their prism glasses would locate him before he made it back to the closest zorg portal located near the hospital. As he ran, his mind went over what happened to his friend. At least Gaul didn't have any kids or a wife to mourn him. Bile was just thankful that he hadn't been the victim. Bile found the storm drain and darted into its depths. He so dreaded reporting back to the Czorg.

Saturday, 11:52 p.m.

Annie had been kept awake by her tormentors since sundown. She had no idea what time it was now. Finally, the two zorgs took a break and locked her in her cell for the night. The jailers were seated at a table in the outer room. She listened to their guttural exchanges and the intermittent sound of something like dice hitting the table. She turned over on the cot to look between the bars at the zorgs. They weren't throwing dice. The objects looked lumpier than dice. It must just be some zorg type of game.

She listened to their guttural exchange, and the intermittent sound of something like dice hitting the table.

Annie was relieved that they finally left her alone! She was not happy. She missed her mom and dad. She thought about the look Jonah had given her dad when they were talking about the beast she had seen. "What would Jonah say to this?" she asked herself, half laughing, half crying. She thought about everything that had come to pass these few last days. She started to say her prayers. She repeated every prayer she could think of over and over, and the effort calmed her down and gave her a sense of peace.

Annie had no idea where Ms. Nichols, Michelle, or Maggie were, but she felt reassured that they were okay. She thought she was the main one the zorgs wanted, anyway. Her wrists ached from the rope that bound them behind her back. Annie arranged her position on the cot so that her back was facing away from the jail door. She had slightly loosened her bounds, and she tried now to clear her backside with the cuffed wrists. The bindings were too tight to allow her to bring her hands to her front.

The scarce light from the distant torch on the wall was waning. Through the bars on the window of the jail, the perfectly round shape of the full moon brightened the nighttime sky. The sound of the objects being thrown on the rock slab and a few raspy words exchanged in the zorg tongue were the only sounds Annie could hear. Her eyes closed as she prayed and fidgeted. She finally found sleep. An occasional sound in the distance would interrupt the silence. Down the hall, the group in the other cell was praying most diligently.

Sunday, 12:16 a.m.

Traveling along the dark palace corridor, Tiggy passed a couple of doorways as he made his way along the hall. He could pick up the scent of Augusta and the girls lingering as he traveled, but he wanted to see what the noise was up ahead. He snuck quietly along. He poked his head low around a doorway and checked out a big room filled with activity. There was a loud din. The room was crowded with zorgs milling about, waiting for something to begin.

Not understanding the language, Tiggy took another calculated look and then scampered back along the corridor to the hallways he had seen earlier. He returned quickly to the very first doorway and turned that way. The cat felt the sway of the triangular piece of glass hanging from his new collar with each step he took.

The minute Tiggy turned the corner he heard the low guttural sounds of two zorgs playing some type of game. The two were seated in a small room at a black slab stone table. They rolled black bones across the table surface. Tiggy crept behind them. Slinking in a dark corner, he watched the creatures. They took turns picking up the objects and dropping them again. One of the zorgs started whining in low guttural tones. The other zorg dozed off right in the middle of the first zorg's tirade. Tiggy knew the signs of nature, including exhaustion. He felt certain that these two disheveled looking rats were tired, very tired. "They aren't up to snuff when it comes to their posts tonight," he thought, which was just fine with him. Somehow he knew that those girls and his master, Augusta, were somewhere around, and he intended to find them.

The first zorg reached over and swatted the head of the dozing drone. He had been snoring. If the Czorg caught them playing this game of bones, or knew that his feeble-headed partner was napping, it would be their end! The second zorg opened his eyes and ran a bony set of claws across his face, shaking his head to help himself wake up from the illegal sleep. The first zorg felt a yawn and slapped his own face to counteract his sudden tiredness.

With the grand convention in progress down the hall, every zorg in the region had been called to attend, other than those on special missions, and the skeleton crew on patrol. Tonight the Czorg and his council would try to come up with a defense strategy against the elf-human alliance.

Weaze and Fruck looked at each other to decide whose turn it was to roll, and again, Fruck's head dropped. He began to snore. Weaze, irritated, prepared to slap the sleeper but instead he found a cozy place for his own head. He would just take a short little nap. He could barely keep his eyes open.

Tiggy, perched nearby, realized that these tired vermin had just bowed out for some sleep. Tiggy had no idea that the influence of the tiny little prism worn on his collar had the same effect on zorgs as Kryptonite had on Superman. Tiggy emerged from his position and nimbly crept along the dark wall past the sleeping guards. He could pick up the scent of a human over the stench of this jail and the stinky zorgs.

The feline saw the prison bars that reflected light cast by a torch mounted on the wall. He walked through the doorway and could make out the shape of someone behind the bars. Slipping easily through the spaces between the bars, the cat moved closer to the sleeping shape. He recognized his master's new friend. He jumped up on the cot where the girl lay and walked over the small shape. A very low "meow" was the sound that Annie heard when her eyes opened. She had been trying to loosen her roped hands until she fell asleep. The cat was now consoling the prisoner. Tiggy obviously realized the danger that she was in. In the darkness he found the ropes on her hands and began to gnaw away at them.

Weaze lifted his heavy head and looked down at the table. His fist still held the bones for the next throw of the game. Somehow he must have fallen asleep. He was so tired. Fruck was asleep. They were going to be dead if they couldn't fulfill their duties, but Weaze felt so tired. It was the sort of tired he usually felt after eating too much for dinner. He swung his head to the right and forced his eyes to do the same. He thought he saw the faint shape of something weird. "Nah!" he thought, and he fell back into a deep, deep sleep.

Tiggy, gnawing away, noticed the recent stirrings at the guards' post and stopped chewing for a moment until the guard fell back to sleep. The cat began working at the girl's bindings again. *"Tiggy is the best!"* Annie remembered Ms. Nichols saying. Annie completely agreed with her. "But how did Tiggy get here?" Annie tried to figure out the mystery until her tired eyes closed. She fell into unconsciousness as Tiggy worked away at her bindings.

Weaze was having a dream. In the dream, a big tiger-striped cat was gnawing away at the ropes on the wrists of the human girl.

Sunday, 3:29 a.m.

John had taken a course on how to escape netting. This class was first given to the soldiers fighting in the Vietnam War. He had never needed to use the knowledge until now. At the time that he took the class, it was required, although most of the men felt that it was just more useless knowledge. Only a handful of people had ever needed to escape from this remote method of capture. Now, he was positively thankful for that education. He learned that the trick for escaping the net was to begin in one place. Do not thrash about. Instead, focus on one spot and eventually, the weave would gradually give way to a larger and larger hole.

The two zorgs dead at either side of his trapped body were enough to make him vomit. "The stench of a dead zorg is ten times the stench of that of a dead human or animal," he thought. Keeping his mind on what he needed to get done, he worked into the wee hours of the morning.

Zorgs occupy the forest at night, as creatures who love to do their deeds by dark. John was apprehensive that he would be discovered before he got away. In the distance he heard the occasional rumblings of an explosion and drums. His nimble fingers finally broke through the strong net. He worked frantically to loosen it enough to reach his knife. Once he got to the knife he would be free. Twisting about, he brought his leg slightly forward and continued to gradually move his arm towards the pocket that held the knife.

He consciously had to fight the panicky feeling of being bound. Working diligently, the hole grew. Finally John was able to get to the knife in his pocket. His fingers encircled the handle and he drew it from the pocket. His thumb found the blade release button, and he heard a clicking sound. His blade was open! Twisting the knife in his hand, the hole tore open and his arm was freed. The knife flew over the strands in a fury. In one final motion, the soldier spread his arms wide and the few remaining strands that kept him bound broke loose. He got to his feet, bent down and sliced the remaining cords. He peeled the net from his body and stepped free.

 The ex-professional soldier gathered up the tattered net and bunched it up as best as he could. Reaching into the thick underbrush, he pushed the bundled material down into the shadows so that it was forced under low branches. John hoped to keep any passing zorgs from seeing the evidence of an escape. Next, he grabbed the two dead zorgs by their legs. He needed to remove the smelly bodies from the trail. He took the first one and swung it over his head, releasing the stinking body and watching it sail into the moonlit darkness. Then he did the same thing with the second creature. "Good riddance!" he said softly to himself, hoping they would never be seen by the enemy.

 His thoughts were now focused on trying to save the girls and Augusta from the jerk rats that called this place home. Moving deftly through the heavy growth, the soldier found himself on a trail. The moon overhead gave him light by which to travel. He stepped to the side of the trail and traveled in the direction of the palace. He was thankful for the vision he was given by the circling eagle when he first arrived before the sun had gone down the previous evening.

Sunday, 4:51 a.m.

Paul was pumped-up about the impending attack. The team was comprised of Navy SEALs, Green Berets, and some expert Air Force personnel. Paul was glad that he had been chosen for this mission. He loved the adrenaline rush of military life, even though his wife said she would be happy when his twenty years were over. The special equipment for this offensive was on its way, being transported by a string of convoy trucks. His friend's home town, Battle Fork, was the headquarters for this mission. According to the reports passed around the staff office overnight, no machinery requiring electricity, gasoline, or battery power would work in this other world realm. Headquarters decided to mount modified ballast tanks filled with the antidote and specially fitted spray rods onto glider planes, instead. They hoped to assemble the planes in the other realm, through the portal located somewhere in the woods along the river. The Army located two planes suitable for the job two states away. They military transported them to the military base two hours away. Both planes should be arriving in their own convoy soon.

Eight convoy vehicles brought troops for the offensive. These noble men had been hand-picked, but would have no knowledge about this operation until their arrival. As they arrived, the soldiers were scanned for the tell-tale zorg tattoo. Paul was shocked to hear that one of the officers, and two soldiers had the zorg mark, and were arrested on the spot. Who could have foreseen this day?

The plan was to spray the zorgs' palace in the nether world with antidote as quickly as possible. The offensive would begin at first light. A zorg had been captured only last night at Chief Graham's police station. There had been three agents working in an office when one of the agents spotted a zorg slinking around the corner to the kitchen. The zorg almost died from the injury caused by an agent that threw a salt shaker and hit the thing in the head, knocking him unconscious. The last Paul heard, the specimen had been transported to one of the government labs for study.

All military personnel would be required to wear a holster carrying a fern sprayer filled with the antidote. Any more attacks by zorgs could best be handled with this spray. Paul remembered the bulletin that said Jesus' name would provide protection, and the Lord's Prayer somehow decreases a zorg's strength significantly. "What would all the lawyers fighting against prayer in school or any public place think about this development?" he thought. Paul, having a strong relationship with Jesus Christ, felt like a version of David who courageously battled the Philistines. "I know God is on my side, and may His will be done," he silently prayed.

The supply trucks had almost all arrived. Paul walked the perimeter of the temporary camp. The soldiers readied their fern sprayers, a couple of the men were saying the Lord's Prayer aloud. More than a few eyes were lifted to the skies. The men still needed to wait until daybreak to find the tracks that led to the portal. If they tried to scout out tracks without enough light, they might ruin them.

In a perfect scenario, the zorgs would be attacked by surprise. The gliders would disinfect the palace of the zorgs that hopefully contained the Czorg, and remaining zorgs would be hunted down by special forces. All of this would take place within two hours, before the first community church services. Certainly, several citizens must have wondered why the army trucks had convoyed down the highways and freeways during the dead of night. Luckily, though, it was early Sunday morning and most people were in bed asleep. The government wanted to keep the operation as secret as possible, especially to assess the zorg threat in greater detail, and then to accurately inform the public. Government officials were rightly concerned about mass hysteria.

Paul walked to the RV to get a fresh cup of coffee. The innocent-looking recreational vehicle was actually a command center filled with surveillance equipment used by Homeland Security to track potential terrorists. He sat down for a few minutes to visit with the personnel and asked if they had heard anything new from headquarters. They told Paul that the zorg injured at the police department had died only minutes ago, and they just started an autopsy.

Paul again refilled his coffee cup. He took off the prism glasses because the steam from the coffee fogged them up. The atmosphere was tense as the trained personnel focused on the heat sensing equipment, trying to discern the presence of any zorgs among the soldiers in the camp. After a few minutes inside the mobile home, Paul went back outside. He put his glasses back on, taking a minute to focus in the dim light.

When the rays of light became bright enough, it would be his job to locate the portal. He was one of the team's principal scouts, but he would also lead a squad to form a perimeter of the palace and exterminate any escapees from the palace.

The soldiers were still unloading the equipment using a forklift that had been sent with the supplies. Soldiers carried the rest of the smaller things and piled the supplies in neat stacks in the main clearing. A spotlight was set up in the work area.

Paul watched as two groups of soldiers began assembling the gliders. Once the planes had been put together, the teams disassembled them again, in practice. The men preparing the ballast tank sprayers checked and re-checked their equipment, adjusting their spray nozzles for accuracy, and then practicing shooting targets with their sprayers filled with water.

Paul had never been on such a strange mission. He leaned against a tree and heard the sound of another truck arriving. He watched a group of soldiers as they unloaded the five gallon jugs of antidote and then carried them on their shoulders to the supply area. He thought to himself that he was glad that he wouldn't have to carry the heavy items through the portal.

The brass called all personnel for a last minute briefing just as the sun began to brighten the eastern horizon. The commanding officer sent Paul and two members of his team to find the portal's location. It was getting brighter by the minute. Paul advanced first and the other men fanned out to the sides of him, looking for clues. Almost immediately they came upon the slight path recently traveled by Chief John Graham and the missing group of civilian's hours before. There were traces of smaller prints beneath the larger prints made by Chief Graham.

Paul and his teammates followed the trail for a few more minutes, moving slowly, carefully. They continued traveling farther to the north. It was easy to find the cottonwood tree and portal entrance. On the ground near the crack in the base of the tree lay a police radio with its curly cord microphone and a police model flashlight, neatly flagging the correct portal position. Paul sent one of his fellow scouts back to the camp to inform his superiors of the portal's position. He directed the other scout to stay posted at the base of the huge cottonwood tree. He followed the instructions given the previous evening by his friend John, and leaned into the center of the old tree. Suddenly, Paul emerged from where moments before he had been, and now found himself looking into the eyes of an attentive elf.

"I'm Andy." He saluted Paul. Paul shook his hand. Andy continued, "My comrade, Gary, was called to the castle during heavy battle last night. Before he left he informed me that your friend, Chief Graham, had come here yesterday evening and that he had requested help from your world in our battle against the zorgs. He then re-entered this realm and went to search for the missing group of humans. We are in desperate need of your help. John and the others haven't returned. We elves continued to fight an intense battle with a number of zorgs we stumbled across during the night and renewed fighting could break out again at any second."

Paul told Andy that he had come to scope the area before bringing in supplies for battle. It was Paul's job to test the wind speed this early morning in the new world, to be sure that the glider planes would properly fly. He would also look for dark surfaces or crops of rocks that would absorb heat and create thermals, or updrafts, used to maintain a glider's altitude. Andy guided him out onto the trail and led him a short distance. Paul noted the wind velocity was nearly perfect for the weight of the planes they would be using. The elf gave Paul a brief description of the surrounding area, including the zorgs' palace location, and where the elves' castle was located. He escorted Paul a short way down the trail, pointing out on the hillside, not far from the mouth of the portal, an ideal spot to launch a glider plane.

A big bird circled overhead, calling out loudly at an intruder in the woods. Paul had read in his report from John's findings the previous evening that the animals here were friendly towards the forces of good. Paul suddenly received an impression, like an intuition, of a big valley. He concentrated on the thought. It was as if the bird was projecting what he was seeing into Paul's thoughts. Paul could see the lay of the land. Paul told Andy he was receiving a vision, and the elf said he'd caught the same thought transference sent by the eagle.

A black palace and a golden colored castle placed themselves in stark contrast on opposite sides of the valley. As he further explored the vision before him, he saw himself and Andy as two small specks below the branches of the tree where they stood. He could also see a zorg perched in a tree near the path down below, behind a crop of trees. He spotted the dark palace on the adjoining hillside and knew the dark color and rocky outcrop would create perfect conditions for the required thermals necessary to sustain the flight of the gliders. Paul was satisfied that the operation was in good shape to proceed.

Just as Paul and Andy turned back towards the portal, they encountered a large white dog with a golden brown collie face and mane. This dog was one of several whose job it was to patrol the wooded area. The dog greeted Andy and introduced himself to the human as Hank. Paul realized that he was somehow able to communicate with the dog. Hank said he had been on this same path the previous day about an hour before dusk when the elves received word of an impending zorg offensive in the valley. Later, after the girls were sent back to the exit portal, he saw signs of a struggle and capture. He had followed the tracks made by the victims and they led to the palace. Late last night, while making the rounds, he had found two dead zorgs in the woods near signs of a disturbance on the path. The man's prints were visible, and a snip of netting lay nearby where evidence of the struggle remained. The dog suspected that the man had escaped. Hank followed the man's tracks right up to the palace gate.

Hank told Paul and Andy he'd reported to the castle guard that the people didn't make it out of the valley. Every able-bodied cat, elf, dog and bird was caught up in the battle near the black palace, and none had located the young group of girls or Augusta. Paul scratched the big dog behind the ears and gave him a piece of beef jerky that he had in his pocket.

Hank gulped down the morsel and told Paul telepathically that he had never before tasted anything so delicious. Paul handed a piece of the jerky to Andy and had a bite himself. Paul and Andy told the dog they saw a zorg hiding in the trees down the path, but they wanted to keep out of sight of the zorg until they were ready to launch their attack. The dog promised to go around the location to avoid being seen, then said goodbye and continued on his way to complete his patrol.

Time was precious. The two went back to the portal. Andy immediately prepared a message for the elders. He sent word to the castle that human re-enforcements would soon arrive and they had already sent a scout to research plans for the human assault on the zorgs' palace. Andy warned them of the zorg hiding near the portal. After placing the message into the small pouch, he placed it on a messenger pigeon's leg and released the bird. Andy then assisted Paul back through the portal.

Back again in the woods he'd left not long ago, Paul found the military troops gathered and preparing the equipment for transport. Several men were balancing glider parts where they stood, waiting for the command to proceed. Paul knew that everyone was energized and ready to go. The sun was bright enough to proceed. Paul radioed the command post and informed them of the new information. They ordered Paul to begin the movement of materials through the portal.

Paul signed off the radio. He warned the men of the spy-zorg he'd seen through the vision sent by the bird, and gave the order to begin moving the equipment. Some of the men went through the entrance to the other world first with smaller parts, so that they became familiar with the destination of the materials. The clearing was out of the line of sight from the zorg's spying eyes because of the line of trees further down the hill. The men began to haul in the heavier items.

The men moving the airplane wings worked in tandem and discovered the best way to send these parts through the portal. It took some practice to get the method down. They worked in pairs, eventually perfecting the moves needed to feed the wings through the small portal, by holding the wings vertically and sending them through to the tall ceilinged portal office. Bulkier metal framework was passed through also, without incident. Finally, the men were able to ship the modified ballast tanks through the portal.

The last items brought through the reality seam were the large jugs of pre-made antidote, carried on the hulking shoulders of the soldiers assigned to this task. Paul supervised the transport process. Once the parts had all been moved, he returned to the hillside where the crew was already piecing together the first glider.

Two men lifted one of the ballast tanks and held it in place while the mechanic tightened the steel bands that secured it. The personnel hoisted the full jugs of the antidote and filled the tanks that had been mounted to the aircraft. Two attachments with nozzle guns were installed, so that attending gunners could strike singular subjects that might try to escape the showering spray of antidote released by the main sprayer nozzles located beneath the wings. The plane could shoot at small targets, or spray over large areas. The first plane was finalized. In no time the second plane would be completed.

While the area buzzed with the necessary activities, it was eerily silent. The operation was conducted in hushed tones. Andy, the portal sentry, had sent dispatches by way of pigeon, keeping the elders at the castle abreast of developments on the hill.

Magnus arrived and gave the men some battle tips. "We are trying to keep the zorgs as busy as we can. I don't think they know you are here yet, but I am sure that very soon they will. Keep your prisms handy. Although you don't need the prisms to see the zorgs in this dimension, they significantly weaken zorg strength. We will send elves out with you. You can't use your radios here, but we elves will carry flags as we fight next to you. When an elf signals, the birds will pick up the image and telepathically communicate it to all other elves needing the information. If you have masks, wear them. Dead zorgs really stink. Always watch your surroundings. Zorgs can easily sneak up on you. If you get caught, pray like crazy. Don't be afraid of the animals. The cats, dogs and birds are all on our side. Feel free to ask them for help. They may not speak English, but they will probably be able to figure out what you need."

Magnus spoke again to the crowd of eager men, ready for battle, and now better prepared for some of the oddities of this realm. It was now time for his pep talk. "Humans, you don't know how long the elven nation has awaited your assistance in ridding the earth of the awful zorg infestation. It is a pleasure to work with you. I know you are here to help us do the right thing. So, do the right thing, and do it quickly. We look forward to helping you in any way we can." Magnus shook Paul's hand.

By now, more than two hundred troops had arrived, prepared for battle. The various teams carried spray bottles of the antidote. Each of the soldiers had a prism in his uniform pocket. The troops' rations included a two day supply of food and water (just in case), a wind-up type watch, and a mirror that they could use to contact the lookout point for the base during the daytime. The troops had all been provided with a sprayer filled with the antidote, worn on a holster on the belt. The bottles full, along with all the soldiers' other supplies, weighed about as much as the radio packs that the personnel had left behind in the human world. The troops were ready to proceed.

The order was given to two Navy SEALs to kill the zorg perched in the tree line. Observers had kept a watchful eye on the spy to note his activities. Maybe it was because of all of the prisms the soldiers carried as they entered the portal, but the zorg wasn't doing his job. He was fast asleep.

Sunday, 4:49 a.m.

John's path became clearer as the forest thinned. He first glimpsed a silhouette of the tower and then the shape of the palace in the shadows up ahead. Escaping that net had taken hours during the dead of night. He prayed he was not too late! As he drew closer, the moon revealed the shape of the palace as it stood eerily in the silence of the early morning darkness. John crept close enough to watch the castle and waited as he had been trained, taking in the situation. He observed the watch-zorg as he made his rounds of the palace, passing near the soldier's lookout.

The zorg sentry made another round before John darted across the clearing to the dark doorway. The door was slightly open! He crept inside and peered down the dark hallway. He saw a few burning torches used to illuminate the place during the night. There were no signs of zorgs nearby. The soldier, at risk of discovery, took a match and lit it close to the ground. It was a dirt and rock floor. John spotted what appeared to be cat prints in the powdery dirt in the match light. "Did the cat make it this far?" he asked himself. He put the light out as quickly as he lit it.

John proceeded down the hallway, avoiding the dim lights from the wall torches as much as possible. He saw a doorway up ahead. Creeping to the opening, he tucked as closely as possible to the wall. He peeked around to look. There were two zorgs at a table in the distance. He watched the two and realized that they were both asleep. The table before them had some little objects on it. John decided to check further down the main hallway. He crept along the same route that his feline friend had taken a few short hours ago. He heard the sounds of the convention down the hall a lot later than his friend, but the cat had much better ears. John inched towards the convention hall as close as he felt was safe. From his hiding place, he observed hundreds of agitated zorgs rambling on in some strange dialect. John knew the zorgs had only one item of business: war.

If only John could get the crew that he had requested to this very place in time, maybe the humans could trap them while the zorgs were all gathered in this building A hundred or a thousand zorgs less would be a blessing! He had seen enough. He stealthily retraced his footsteps and soon was at the second hallway he'd passed. He traveled quietly, hugging the wall in the darkness, until he came upon a short hallway off the main corridor leading to a jail station.

The guards in this cell were murmuring to one another. Kazook and Dreeg were soon to be relieved. There were some combat and patrolling zorgs as well as some guard zorgs making up the skeleton crew, but all of the other zorgs in the region were attending the meeting in progress. These two expected to be rotated in, as they had not yet been to the council chambers.

John stood perfectly still, his heart racing. He could see the jail cell with Augusta and two girls, apparently asleep. There should be three girls, but for now John would contend with the immediate problem of releasing the prisoners and doing away with these zorgs quietly in the process. He had no idea that the jailer's schedule would be replacing these two zorgs shortly.

Kazook and Dreeg were trying to prepare the reports they needed to present to the council within the hour. All of the zorgs' long hours had made the two foggy-headed and they kept trying to rewrite the reports to sound intelligent. Not much had been revealed by the questioning of the prisoners, anyway. Not much was expected for tonight. The interrogators were working the prisoners mainly so that by tomorrow they would be more cooperative when questioned before the great Czorg.

Not understanding why, Kazook told his partner Dreeg that he was beginning to feel sleepy, and not too good. Dreeg sat a little farther away from where the ex-Navy SEAL stood motionless by the entrance, in the shadows. The influence of the prism in the soldier's possession had started to wear down the first guard. Soon the second one felt the prism's effect. They would both be helplessly asleep and vulnerable in no time. In a matter of minutes the snoring began. John hoped that the snores would not draw too much attention to the so-called guard post.

He leaped into action, entering the small outer room where the two zorgs slept noisily. On a peg on the wall was a ring of keys. John decided to let the two jailers sleep while he got the girls out, since earlier he'd discovered how much a dead zorg stinks. It might attract unwanted attention before he completed his mission.

John made only a slight noise as he tried the first three keys in the jail cell lock, to no avail. As quietly as possible, he tried the fourth key. The sounds had awakened the captives. Relief flushed across Augusta's face as she realized they were being rescued! The chief of police was more handsome in her eyes now than ever. He sheepishly smiled at the woman in the faintly lit cell, and his heart took a little leap. He furiously tried to hurry.

The door clanked and the bolt lock released. The rusty metal jail door screeched noisily when John pulled it open. He pressed his knife lever, and the blade opened. He cut the cords on their wrists. Augusta ushered the girls out of the small cage and they tiptoed past the still dozing zorgs. The last thing John did as they exited the cell office was to spray a dose of the antidote into the captors' faces. The stink erupted at once. John swung a door shut as he left the place, hoping the stink might be reduced to this room and blocked from the rest of the palace.

John, Augusta and the two cousins tiptoed down the hallway and stayed in the darkness as much as possible. They were hunting for their friend, Annie. Augusta whispered to John that she thought she'd heard Annie's voice coming from the left of where they had been held prisoners. John decided she must be describing the first hall he'd passed, immediately inside the doorway when he entered the palace. Creeping quietly, the girls followed their leader and hoped they could find their friend. Most of all they wanted to escape before the throngs of zorgs somewhere in the palace emerged like kids from an elementary school at three-thirty.

John had his own agenda. Once he found the missing girl and escorted the group back to the safety of the portal and back to the human world, he wanted to get his men into position to poison the beasts' lair while the zorgs were all in it. This opportunity might be short-lived.

Gesturing for the girls to remain where the shadows seemed to converge, John trekked down the hallway alone. He scouted a small room he passed along the way. Nothing in there but chains and supplies for the jail. At the end of the hall was another jailers' room and cell. Once again the two guards were both fast asleep. The dim torch on the wall was burning low and was practically out. It shed enough light for John to spot the cell bed and dark shapes inside.

Just to be safe, he sent a short spray of antidote into the snoring zorgs' faces. They never knew what hit them. He grabbed a ring of keys from a hook and rushed to the jail door. The sounds John made woke the prisoner. It was so dark! Annie was frightened. She hugged the big cat. Tiggy had actually been able to gnaw the binds off of her wrists while she was asleep! Tiggy was her only comfort throughout the long hours. Not knowing yet what the sounds were, Annie scrambled towards the wall, still hugging Tiggy, trying to put as much space between herself and what was coming to get her.

John, trying the second key, identified himself to the moving shapes. He had found the right key and turned it. He opened the door. The cat meowed and Annie, making out the police chief's shape, dropped the cat and hugged John. After the nightmarish experience she'd had, she had never been so happy! He took Annie's hand. She picked up Tiggy with her other arm. They crept past the dead, smelly zorgs. Annie held her breath. She let go of John's hand for a second and grabbed the bone things that the zorgs had used in their game. She wanted a souvenir of her adventure. She popped them into her pocket, taking John's hand once again. The pair made it back to the shadows where the others were waiting. Annie hugged the waiting group and handed Tiggy over to Augusta.

John signaled for the ex-prisoners to swiftly follow, as he led them back through the maze to the back door of the palace. Whispering for the others to wait in the shadows, he slipped out the door to make sure it was clear to bring his group out to safety.

Crouching in the bushes by the corner, he waited for the sentry to make his next round. John pulled the trigger and the wash of mist dropped the zorg where he'd stepped his last. Once again, John grabbed the leg of the zorg and hurled the thing, and it sailed far into the trees.

Back to the doorway in a flash, John whispered impishly, with a smile, "A sail-zorg!" He directed them to follow as he led them away from the black palace and past the very place where he'd been nabbed by the two zorgs the evening before.

John tracked back to where the girls had been kidnapped. In the growing light from the east, John found the hidden gunnysack and handed it to Augusta. Augusta gave Tiggy back to Annie before she took the bag from John. Her hand touched his, and he squeezed it. "Augusta, you don't know how glad I am to see you and the girls safe. I could think of nothing else."

Augusta smiled at the handsome police officer. "John Graham, you are the sweetest sight for sore eyes. The girls and I were so frightened, being held in that dark and smelly place. We feared for

Annie's life. You came to our rescue and saved us! How can we ever thank you?"

John smiled back. "Well, you can. Come out to dinner with me, once this thing is over." Augusta blushed. He turned to the rest of the group. "I want to take all of you girls out for dinner! The pleasure will be mine! You are the heroes here!"

"No, you are the hero," Annie said, as the girls blushed from Chief Graham's compliment. "Now, let's hurry and get out of here, because I don't want to go back to that dungeon." The urgent request startled John out of infatuation and back to reality as he led them forward up the last of the trail. Andy was overjoyed to see them! He met them outside of the entrance.

"John," he said, "everyone is so relieved to see you and the missing captives! Paul, your old buddy from the service, is here. We plan to attack within the half hour. We are so glad that we don't have to prioritize a search and rescue mission over the attack of the zorg palace. Our battle plan was in jeopardy because we didn't know where you guys were.

The returning captives followed him, wide-eyed as military personnel around them worked diligently with the last preparations for war. The planes were ready to fly, and the men and elves waited for the signal. John was quickly absorbed by Paul and other military commanders.

"The zorg convention is still in progress," John noted, "but I don't know for how long. They know you are coming, but obviously don't expect you until at least this afternoon. I was lucky enough to kill the guards circling the castle and the four girls. But there are hundreds, maybe even a thousand zorgs in that palace desperate for human blood. You need to attack, NOW, before it is too late. By the way, the antidote works like a charm." He drew a diagram of the Czorg Palace. "The convention hall has a large fireplace where antidote could be pumped through the chimney…"

Annie was tired. As the four continued the last few yards to the portal, Magnus noticed them. He ran to greet Augusta and the missing girls. He hugged them and said, "Oh, thank God that you are safe! We sent elves out after your disappearance, but we were too late to intercept your capture. I am so glad you are alright! I feel so bad about this! Let's make a point to have a visit, after this is over. We elves are ecstatic that the zorgs didn't get the chance to hurt you, and that your human army is ready to fight!" Magnus beamed!

An officer cut off the conversation. "I hate to hurry you, but we must begin the attack. Two SEALS were sent a short time ago to remove the threat of the zorg look-out fifty yards away. Hopefully, our men were able to stop that zorg before he saw you return and then warn the palace of your escape. It's time to go!" At that, the officer handed the girls off to Andy and asked him to escort the tired ex-prisoners back to the portal and safety.

John's information changed some of the battle plans. A ground and air assault would be conducted simultaneously. One group of soldiers would secure the perimeter around the Czorg's palace, and Paul's regiment of two hundred would infiltrate the castle. The gliders were ready, and would pre-mist the ground with antidote before the zorgs tried to escape. A quick thinking elf suggested filling the pigeon dispatch bags with prisms, and the birds would drop their bags on and near the castle. "Shattered prisms are still prisms, right?" he reasoned.

Still trying to be as quiet as possible, with the soldiers and elves in battle positions, all raised their hands in unison as a battle cry. The sun could barely be seen over the horizon. The gliders went in first. Two elves and two pilots were present on each glider plane. Soldiers on the ground gave the first aircraft a shove and it picked up speed and began to sail. The second plane was launched. The two glider planes silently swirled into the air on currents that carried the planes with invisible fingers. The large number of zorgs inside of the palace would hopefully create strong thermals to allow the planes to elevate, if necessary. The pilots expertly steered their crafts towards the Czorg palace, dousing the castle and surrounding area. Next, the pigeons dropped prisms on the roof and in the chimney of the castle. A low rumble sound emerged from the castle as Paul set out with his team and a group of elven soldiers and, working in twos, scaled the sides of the building carrying ropes. The men attached the ropes to the vents, and threw the makeshift ladders down to the soldiers waiting below. Men climbed the ladders carrying the antidote hoses over their shoulders up to the roof. Working in tandem, they quickly inserted them into the openings on the chimney and vents on the roof. The antidote began spraying through the screens on the tip of each hose, creating a misting effect. The rumble turned into agonizing shrieks. Paul knew the antidote must be doing its job.

The men on the roof held the hoses that released a steady spray of the antidote through the chimney vent system.

Foot soldiers rushed through the doors located on the ground floor of the Czorg palace. These "frontline" soldiers needed extra protection, including a mask and plastic armor to deflect needles, should the mosquito-like zorg noses attempt to sting the human attackers. The soldiers advanced, rushing the corridor, taking the inhabitants by surprise.

The hoses had already pumped a fatal amount of the antidote spray into the zorgs' air supply. The outer fringes of the huge group were unaffected yet by the fumes and tried to escape. Not only did the soldiers have to fight the zorgs, but also the urge to vomit as the zorgs became carcasses. Their yellowish or pinkish white needle noses oozed poison and odor. The soldiers' eyes burned. The crowded hallways were full of soldiers, shoulder to shoulder, carrying spray containers of the antidote. As they advanced, the ongoing spray left piles of the writhing, dying beasts.

The soldiers in the second wave of the attack spread out and systematically closed up the windows. The hand spray from the soldiers, combined with the overhead spray, was filling the palace with the poisonous air. The zorgs twisted and shook in dying spasms. It appeared that the attack was a smashing success!

Sunday, 6:12 a.m.

When Augusta's foot touched on the human plane, a helpful hand took hers and assisted her as she found her footing. A military escort was waiting to greet the returning humans. The group of four was whisked away from the tree portal to the picnic area where they were given the opportunity to freshen up in the comfort of the bathroom of the large recreational vehicle the staff was using for headquarters. The girls took turns calling their families. Annie was so relieved to hear her Mom's voice."

"Honey, are you alright?"

"Mom, I know you think I have a crazy imagination, but even I could not have imagined this. Last night I was kidnapped by a zorg."

"What?"

"Make a cup of coffee for you and dad and come over here, north of town. It will be pretty obvious to figure out where we're at."

Thirty minutes later, after the girls and their parents exchanged hugs, the officer in charge spoke to the parents of the girls. He briefly described their kidnapping, and explained the need for a debriefing session. The four women and Annie and Maggie's parents (Michelle's parents would arrive later in the day) were served a light breakfast of donuts, juice, and fruit in the military hospitality trailer before being whisked off to the closest military base. While they ate, they could hear the sound of a waiting helicopter. They were told that Augusta, Maggie, Michelle, and Annie would be flown to the airbase and then taken by plane to Washington for debriefing. The parents of the girls would go home and pack overnight cases, to be escorted to Washington later in the day. Annie's dad did not approve.

"Sorry sir," the uniformed officer replied. "I am just following orders. Besides, we don't have enough room for all of you. These girls are important to national security right now. And you sir, will be escorted to your home because we feel you might be in danger as well." Annie's dad kissed her goodbye and Maggie's and Annie's parents left with several uniformed men.

Augusta, Annie, Michelle, and Maggie were led outside. The stalks of corn blown to the ground by the helicopter blades made a giant circle. "It looks like a crop circle," Annie thought. One officer helped the girls up through the open door. Another crew member helped the visitors into their seats and fastened their seat belts for them. Annie and the others had never dreamed that they would ride in a helicopter. They settled into their seats and tried to relax, but the energy generated by the activity and danger had everyone in an excited state.

The three girls compared their wrists. They all had sore red marks. Annie rubbed hers gingerly. The red bands represented a badge of honor. She would never be the same again. The things that had happened in the last few days had left her a different person.

Annie closed her eyes and thanked God above for being such a good God. She thought about her time alone the previous night, and knew that even in the danger, she hadn't been alone, nor was she ever alone, but she always had God, no matter what.

She asked the others how they were doing. She looked at Augusta, Michelle and Maggie. She said, "When I was by myself last night, I could feel God's strength and peace over me. I felt that you all were praying for me."

Maggie and Michelle told Annie how the zorgs had questioned them, but he left them in their cell together, and when the zorgs finally left them alone for the night, all three of them had prayed for Annie.

The pilot reminded the group to keep their prism glasses near, since now it was necessary to use them. The helicopter lifted off and headed south. Annie and the girls looked out of the rounded window. The tiny spot of shadow made by the helicopter looked like a traveling dot across the landscape of their little town below. The girls tried to identify their houses and other landmarks.

Annie found her street and saw a police cruiser circling her block. Seeing that, she felt sure that her family was fine. She pointed it out to the others. They in turn noted the patrol car parked in the street near Augusta's and Michelle's houses. Maggie pointed to one parked in front of her house. Maggie thanked God out loud for their families' safety.

Spotting the activities of the early Sunday morning town below them, Augusta pointed out the several churches in the community dotted with church-goers. People were getting out of their cars and walking across the parking lots for the early morning service. "Little do they know," said Annie, "that their prayers couldn't come at a better time."

"Prayers account for so much good that the prayer giver doesn't realize is occurring as a result," said Augusta.

Annie adjusted her prism glasses. She slid down in the seat enough to get her hand into her pocket with the helicopter seat belt left in place. She dug down and retrieved the objects that the zorgs had been tossing across the slab table the evening before. She was glad she snatched them from the dead zorg prison guards. She had a memento of the grueling events. Annie held the odd-shaped game pieces out for the others to see. "I bet this is the last time that my family makes fun of my imagination." She grinned. The others took turns examining the odd items. Annie re-adjusted her prism glasses, then turned in her seat to address the others. "What do you think might be happening right now with John and the soldiers in the other world?"

Augusta said, "Prayer is one thing I do know we can do to help. Let's say a prayer for them all right now. They could use God's help."

The four passengers, along with the pilot and crew all joined in. "Our Father, who art in heaven, hallowed be Thy Name. Thy kingdom come, Thy will be done on earth as it is in heaven. Give us this day our daily bread and forgive us our trespasses, as we forgive those who trespass against us, and lead us not into temptation, but deliver us from evil. For Thine is the kingdom, the power and the glory forever and ever. Amen"

THE END